the
patient
routine

the
patient
routine

by

luna rey hall

"A psychedelic, propulsive stream-of-consciousness narrative that feels at times claustrophobic, at times conspiratorial, and at all times curiously suspenseful. Unlike anything I've ever read."
— Nick Cutter, author of *The Troop*

"Filled with frantic death energy. Entrancing, gruesome, and heartening too. hall's lyrical hospital saga shows that we are small inside the grandiose mortality machine."
— Hailey Piper, Bram Stoker Award-winning author of *Queen of Teeth*

"the patient routine is a merciless, anxiety-charged, possible-apocalypse, possible-zombie thriller, long narrative poem about the body in maddening conversation with itself. luna rey hall takes us through the terrifying halls of a hospital in lockdown while deftly exploring an immensely personal journey through the shifting realities of an over-medicalized mind, a body snared in systems that do not understand or serve it. The tension between inner and outer worlds is relentless and the body horror hits all the worst/best buttons while raising philosophical questions of identity and power. What a torturously smart little book."
— Joe Koch, author of *The Wingspan of Severed Hands* and *Convulsive*

the patient routine

Edited and formatted by Stephanie Ellis

Cover illustration by Elizabeth Leggett
First Edition: June 2023

ISBN (paperback): 978-1-957537-60-3
ISBN (ebook): 978-1-957537-59-7
Library of Congress Control Number: 2023935155

BRIGIDS GATE PRESS
Bucyrus, Kansas
www.brigidsgatepress.com

Printed in the United States of America

Content warnings are provided at the end of the book

contents

02:59 AM   1

04:28 AM   4

04:31 AM   5

04:49 AM   6

05:35 AM   7

05:57 AM   10

06:51 AM   11

07:26 AM   12

07:28 AM   13

07:45 AM   15

08:02 AM   16

08:08 AM   17

08:17 AM   19

08:18 AM   20

08:22 AM   22

08:37 AM   25

08:50 AM   27

09:40 AM   30

09:44 AM   32

09:44 AM   33

09:51 AM   34

10:35 AM   36

10:46 AM   39

10:48 AM   41

10:49 AM   43

10:50 AM   46

10:51 AM   47

11:18 AM   51

11:23 AM   53

contents

11:39 AM	58
11:45 AM	61
11:48	64
1?:50 AM	66
11:56 AM	71
12:04 ?M	74
12:25 PM	79
12:?4 PM	81
XX:XX XX	84
12:37 PM	86
12:43 PM	88
12:4? PM	92
??:58 PM	96
01:?4 PM	101
01:?4 PM	102
??:15 PM	109
0?:2? P?	113
??:26 PM	116
??:2? ?M	119
01:?? PM	122
0?:3? ?M	127
?1:?? ??	129
??:?? PM	133
??:?? PM	134
0?:?2 ??	137
?1:44 ??	143
?1:44:23 ??	144
?1:44:41 ??	145
?1:44:?3 ??	146
?1:44:?? ??	147
?1:44:?? ??	148
?1:44:58 ??	150
?1:44:5? ??	151
0?:?4 ??	154

contents

01:?? PM   158
01:?? PM   159
??:????? ??? ?????? ? ? ??? ? ? ?   163
?1:?4 ??   165
??:1? PM???????   171
??:5? ?????????????????   175
??:?? P?????????????????????????   182
??:?? ??   184
??:?9 ??????????????   185
??:0? ?????   187
0?:?? ?M   189
03:55 PM   196
04:06 PM   198
Acknowledgements   201
About the Author   203
About the Illustrator   205
Content Warnings   207
More from Brigids Gate Press   209

02:59 AM

they say our greatest fears are manifested
right before we slip into sleep.
that twilight period of consciousness.
those brief moments when you aren't entirely sure
whether you're still awake.

when you're most vulnerable.

people often say they can't fall asleep
because they're mulling over worries.
their stress.
                   their anxieties.

Ashton ...

tonguing them into a ball in their mouth.
little dab of gum chewed to death.

well, i don't sleep either.

i don't think of anything in particular though.
i wish i had something to grasp onto.

a thought to stall in my mind.

the image of my teeth rotting,   the festering ooze
        curling around the enamel,   pliers
barging into my mouth

to pull the impacted culprit,
the mastic aftermath.

Ashton …

but it's just me, in this emptiness,
night after night, a monochromatic sea
lapping against a monochromatic sky

& no sound or scent or sea air salt.
nothingness. a void of me & my body.

hyperaware of every little thing.

i don't think the body should be
this focused on itself.

we aren't supposed to feel our heartbeat
like this. our brain should suppress
all the tiny pangs throughout our body
that don't warrant a single thought.

but i'm different.

i'm constantly thinking of every inch of me.

every little spasm & movement & dullness & cleft & pulse & drift
& blur & sting & hollow-
ing— filling— accumulating shit.

it's like someone forgot to flip off my switch
& then removed it entirely.

there hasn't been a day that i'm not
in this constant state of awareness.

Ashton …

every detail of my body repeating over & over.

feeling the way an eyelid sits over the eye.
feeling the way my toes, one toe— really,
makes a cracking noise when i move it.
feeling a sting under the thumb,
the way my cock is a little hard,
the shaved itch on top of my feet,
the prick in my ear,
the prick in my other ear,
the prick in my armpit, the sharp prick
along my spine, down the small
of my back &—

Ashton …

what?

stop monologuing …
you aren't worth it …

—eventually, i fell asleep.

04:28 AM

& then i awoke.

skin drenched in pre-dawn sweat. teeth still firmly
rooted in my mouth. odor-producing bacteria
breaking down the morning air.

i was left with a nightmare
saturated & stretched over a firmament
of star remnants. a dead glow,
hunk of ash. papule sky.

meaningless nothingness.

mortared into an anxious arrhythmic
pattering.
throbbing within the skin.

a fear that something much worse

may be lingering deep
within the blood. a tangle;
roots drinking thirsty
in a field of rot.

04:31 AM

& then, i went back to bed.

blanket over my head. calico cat hair all snarled
in the fabric. CPAP nasal mask a full gasp of air.

fall.

fall.

let the eyes tire, let the body still itself.
let the mind vanish
into the nether. a vortex of disassociation.

sleep.

sleep.

sleep.

sleep.

please, sleep.

what's that?

tiny pain. a swell.

a bead behind the left ear.

crescendo. occipital shock.
the tossing & turning.
a churning.

what's that?

04:49 AM

what's that, Ashton?

my eyes pried open.
soft hand behind the ear,
digging behind the lobe.
the shadow of pain.

i needed to get up.
to examine.
it had to be worse
than i was thinking but …

but what?

i swung my body, legs dangled off the bed,
feet not touching the ground
until i pulled a clean pair of socks
from the nightstand & slipped them on.

felt the bump by the ear one more time
before i noticed the sunlight drip down
the wall through the curtain sway.

i've been awake
for too long already.
it's morning,

isn't it?

my five senses: all plagues of worry.

05:35 AM

sometimes you look at yourself as that plague of worry
                                      & you see
                        another.

someone capable of surviving.
capable of thriving, a whole garden.
i hope to see that in myself
one day
but right then,

i was a flesh-bag swallowed by disease.

           it must
                 be disease.

how could it be
anything
else?

                                       do you see the bump?
neck craned in the mirror to reveal the bulge under my ear.

                                           it's something.

i knew it was something
but who would have believed me
when my own eyes were seeing a pristine,
lotioned, gentle-rubbed veneer of skin?
pain can't always be seen, right?

right.

i moved my hand over, thumb
rubbing against the tender spots.
masseter strung up in tension
pinched down with all the strength of the jaw.

of all my symptoms
this one bugs me the most.

bug.

could it be a bug?
an insect burrowed into my skin.

it could be.

couldn't it?

i needed to be skillful.
finger under my nose to feel the air.
that cool push from the nostrils.
an attempt to catch my breathing,
calm. pulled my hand away,
what else do i need to feel?

breathe.
breathe.

remember what your therapist told you.

what did my therapist tell me?

let's continue with our day.
worrying about it won't solve anything.
let's continue with our day.

the way wind pushed through leaflets & bracts,
the inflorescences when it hit
the dogwoods outside my bedroom window.

05:57 AM

when the sun hit those dogwoods i knew
i had class in two hours.
college sophomore. just started.

                                              "i'm
                                          only 19.
                         i can't be dying,
can i?

"i'm only 19.
                    i've done nothing.
                                 is this
                               really my
                               time?

                                    "i'm
                    only
19."

i should call my mama.
see what she thinks.
ask her if i should be worried,
like i did when i was a kid.

06:51 AM

i called my mother,   my sister,
        my ex-partner,
called just about   anyone
& not one of them really listened.

not like when you listen in the morning,
coffee up in your nostrils, a single chirp
at the deck window & you really listening
to find out if that's the same sparrow
as the day before.

that kind of listening.
                        not a one of 'em.

07:26 AM

so, what was i to do?
i needed someone to listen.

Ashton, i'm here, let's look at this
l
o
G
i
c
a
L
l
Y.

07:28 AM

logically,

yes logically:

we googled what ailed me.
checked all my symptoms.

it may be better to list the ones
i don't have but here goes—

an ad pop-up.

Non-Hodgkin's Lymphoma Or Chronic Lymphocytic Leukemia?
Compensation May Be Available!

—i've never been tested for either of those.
i can't receive compensation
without a diagnosis.

any of these symptoms match?

racing heart, check. feeling weak,
oh yeah, dizzy, yup, faint, possibly.
i have never fainted so how would i know?
but yes, faint,

faint for sure.

tingling, where?
tingling everywhere. & a numbness, yes.
quite numb. hands, feet, elbows.

should i be feeling
my elbows? look at how i'm sweating.

carpet a makeshift pool now.
so cold. it's like my body's
thermometer cracked. i couldn't breathe,
my chest hurt, i wasn't in control anymore.

no?

all from a bump.

all from a bump.

but it's so much more.

so much more.

the sense that something terrible is about to happen.

ah, impending.

the sense that i'm falling apart.

i need help.

~~help~~.

that's enough reason   to worry.

07:45 AM

that was enough reason to worry so,
i entered my Buick. a death trap— all cars.
stepping into a vehicle is asking for a grave.
a mobile prayer for the end.

started the ignition, engine rolled over, purr sweet.
the wheels glided across left-behind puddles.

it had been storming. eyesore lightning creased
over the pitch-dark clouds, eardrums
menaced by thunder's bleat.

but everything that morning was peace,
neighbor tended her garden,
hands along the stems
making sure they weren't too bent,
beaten by last night.

i think, i drove past too fast
to make sure myself ...
but, oh— stop sign.

there was a stop sign.
slow down. please,

                                        i couldn't get
                              killed

on the way to my dying.

08:02 AM

getting killed on the way
to dying
would have been just like me.   *totally.*

as i blinkered into the ER parking lot,
i noticed the cumuli-underbellies still heavy
with pending inundation. an uneasy fog

coughed out along the horizon
of the hospital. air crisp, waiting.
a nipping chill & exposure.

the perfect kind of weather.

08:08 AM

"… you heard that right, the perfect kind of weather.
mid-60s. sunny, with a cool bre—"

weatherpeople are always liars, especially on television,
especially on hospital sets. the lobby vestibule
brisked kind of empty, late-Fall tree empty.
a little too empty for my taste, a little too full
at the same time.   *which?*

i stumbled around the entrance, moved aside for someone
being brought in on a wheelchair. their face creole marble;
blues & yellows crossed under the off-white. worn. old.
if only i looked so worn, such an aged, malfunctional body.
a gradual withering.

senescence in my palm.

watched them at the counter then i hit up the restroom.
no need to look for a sign.

i feel as comfortable here as i do at home.
splashed my face with water. that neutral temp.
the blonde ends of my hair. split. brunette center.

mirror reflected the dark crescents under my eyes.
really if you think about it, what could be the problem?
                                                                            logically.

logically, yes, so logically— wait let's see
if the drive helped. felt the node again,
it feels   *different.*
yeah, different. the drive did not help.
if anything,

                                                        driving made
                                                        it worse.

08:17 AM

driving made it so much worse; i should tell my health team.
"flared up under driving conditions," maybe that would help them
pinpoint the cause. give them something
to put under the microscope.

ok, just: leave the restroom, hands dried
                                       twice.
nails bristled with the thin side
of the brown paper-towels. cheap shit.

exit. wiped my hands one more time
on my sweatpants. smears of wet along gray fleece
when i approached the counter, there was still
a blade of water between two of my fingers.
there's a thin plastic sign on the front side
of the counter that i used to remove the remnants of liquid.

rubbed my webbing dry. the receptionist lifted their head.
ears held down by large sun earrings. horrifyingly large.
though, i liked the way they did their hair. curled bun.
their name was Mabel. a name tag, a nameplate.

they'd never say it but i could tell they didn't want to see me.
not here, not then. not again.
that knowing look people give:

why'd it have to be you?

08:18 AM

why

    did it

        have to be

                you?
                Ashton.
                Ashton.
                Asht—

"sir, how can i help you?" their voice
a dull siren. sterilized of all comfort.

                sir?

"sir?" i responded. "oh, hello, i'm having
a medical emergency, i think."

"okay, Mr. Reed, please fill out that form," a clipboard
with papers clipped scuffed across the counter's surface.
"we'll be sure to attend to you as quickly as possible."

as quickly …   but
                        you can't
                        outrun

                        death.

"i'm dying,"

i told her. as if that would trigger a different response.
a flurry of antibodies & sepsis. to tell the staff:

this time i meant it. "i'm dying," i said again.
my voice light helium, neoprene smooth. squeaky.

so is
every-
one
else.

all the other patients each had their own tragedy.
their own emergency. that cough, that bruised skin,
that child crying into their hands, mother next to them,
where was the other parent? where are my parents?

alone. all their eyes were on me
as i hesitated to grab the clipboard.

"i understand, Mr. Reed. please take the form,
we can't see to you until you let us know
what's wrong. please fill out the form."

08:22 AM

the form:

[date]	09/22/2021
Ashton Reed	[name]
[ID]	?????????
11/17/2001	[D.O.B.]
[sex]	...
...	[sex]
[sex]	...

heart rate:	?
?	: blood pressure
respiratory rate:	?
	: temp.
weight: *oh!*	186
5'10"	: height

"family history"

	mother's side:	father's side:
i don't know who did what.		*what should you put?*
high blood pressure:	i don't know	i don't know
cholesterol:	no,	i don't know
...:	i don't	know
heart disease:		idk
...:		
obesity:	i don't know	maybe

diabetes: idk   i do not know
cancer: YES   i don't know
…:   i said, i don't know
alcoholism: idk   idk
mental illness:

"cause of death"
            of grandparents,
                        parents
                                    or
                              siblings

                                    i don't
                              know …

"medical history"

stroke? heart disease? ✓ high blood pressure? ✓ (i think)
diabetes? arthritis? ✓ (i think) seizures? mental illness?
no! depression? ✓ (yes, the counselor said)
kidney disease? cancer? ✓ (active, non-diagnosed)
                                                      100%
100%
bleeding disorder? ✓ (i have bled before, yes)
alcoholism ✓
                                            (what defines that?)
lung diseases? tuberculosis? ✓ (i may have, how
would i know?) anemia? ✓ obesity? stomach ulcers? ✓
(maybe) liver trouble? ✓ (trouble)
thyroid trouble? ✓ (trouble) HIV/AIDS?

other. other. other. other. other. other.   *other?*
D, all of the above.

        [are you on any medication?]
        yes

        [if Yes, list medications]
        i can't remember

        [have you had surgery before?]
        maybe? i don't remember much
        before today.
        right now.

        [if Yes, explain]
        i told you.
        i don't
        remember
        much
        before today.

        [allergies]
        not that i know of.

        is that enough?
        [okay, now:
        reason for current visit]

08:37 AM

the reason.

the reason.

the reason. for my current visit is …

   [what is your primary problem?]
   colossal pain. a fist behind my left ear.
   bursting seams. mawkish taste
   on my tongue. febrile firestarter.
   no,
   more than that.

   [what are the symptoms?]
   i said …
   colossal pain.

         worry.
   fever,
   seriously
   bloated flesh, behind my left ear.

   i'm plump ready to pop. a botfly,
maybe,
   another insect, insects. teeming
underneath
   the skin. knuckles rolling under a
blanket.

   i'm a hive. but if you can't find
anything

like that then i need a scan, any
kind will do.
          maybe it's cancer.

[have you ever had a similar
problem]
like this? exactly like this?

no.

[if Yes, how long
a

g

o

?

]

N/A

[are there any other problems
we should be aware of today?]
other problems …

[if Yes, list problems]

problems …
problems …
problems …
problems …

other problems.
let me think on that for a moment.

08:50 AM

all the problems, all mine.

all yours.

a hoarder of trauma.

"hello," Mabel— "did you finish filling out the form?"
i had been zoned out, swaying while a couple
formed a line behind me.

"i'm not sure there is enough room for all my problems."
my laugh hoarse. that scritch, airy kind.
they didn't laugh though, perhaps internally,
sometimes i laugh internally when i don't want others
to know what i think is funny. i guess people
don't really laugh at my jokes all that often.
considering the majority of people i talk with are simply
obligated to because they are in healthcare
& i'm always within healthcare.
maybe it's something with my delivery.

"well, we'll take a look, Mr.
Reed & i'll be sure to let the next available nurse know."

"but, uh, & i don't mean to be a bother so early
in the morning but it's really an emergency.
i wouldn't be surprised if i didn't keel over."
spaced, off in the distance, their eyes drifted southeast.
"maybe Dr. Reynolds could see me. sooner rather than later."

she, Dr. Reynolds, understands my current situation. she's a saint.
i've been with her for years.   *really?*

"she is currently busy with other patients, so as per usual,
you will need to wait. i'm sure she'll be happy to see you
when the time comes." their fingers a signal to the others
in the waiting room. like i'm just another patient here.

everyone with their eyes all riveted on me.
like i'm insane. but come on, have you seen me? "okay, sure,
just let her know what i said, the whole emergency thing."

"of course, Mr. Reed."

i nodded & strolled, with a hint of pride that i stood up for
myself,
to a seat isolated enough from others to maintain a good safe
distance.
before sitting down, i sifted my pocket for a wipe & cleaned
the seat of ass sweat & little dusties. i'd do a better cleanse
when i grab some supplies from the bathroom. next trip.

mr.

mr.

mr.

tsk.
tsk.

tsk.

my leg radiated. up & down, up & down. enraptured
by its own anxious engine. real rebarbative so i tried to stop it.
grabbed the thigh right above the knee.

i needed to see Dr. Reynolds.

09:40 AM

& that's when the hermetic doors pried open & medical staff
barreled out, pressurized springs. rounding the trail end,

Dr. Reynolds. in all her sweet latex. face a beautiful
plastic shield & goggles. the way she walked to the front desk.
the other staff with their maudlin tones. all of them humming
from the nectar of a … a successful procedure.

maybe. she grabbed some papers from a tray
before giving a look over her shoulder

at me,   *i'm sure—*
& when she did, the emergency entrance orifice snapped open.
a flurry of automatic breath: the softest, quickest whoosh
followed by a complete & utter silence. no room for an incision
of heartbeat, cough, or mastication or— my thoughts dulled to a
focus:

a single stretcher wheeled in by two medics
on either side & on either side that i looked,
the person on the stretcher looked deader than dead.

like i might be in a few minutes. the way i reflected
in the set-aside pair of glasses next to their head.
latticework of veins softening the skin blue.
that five-day bristled chin, the straps to hold them
in place, the regular clothes, the regular pain,
they looked no different from anyone else here.

yet all the rush & energy surrounding their arrival
was anything but regular. at least, no different
that i could see. from this distance. but the odor
did penetrate my nostrils & several others
as they revolted in their seats. this sweet, rotten smell.
old meat. an immediate sour aftertaste.

i couldn't help but retch. my mouth sweating with pre-vomit.
& as quickly as they entered, they vanished back
into the intensive care unit. straight to an operating room,
i assumed. the whole time, Dr. Reynolds had this perplexed
cerulean look to her eyes. then she noticed me.

the way she smiled.

09:44 AM

suddenly her smile vanished, like all my symptoms
for that brief moment, when i approached.

at her side within an instant but at her side
always, really. my guide. "oh, Ashton.
i didn't know you were here today. i'm so—"

"i know we always keep meeting each other
like this. here, at this hospital." the way my eyelids flared;
pupil point expanded. dashed in the fluorescents.
the jitter of my affection.

"well, yes, that is certainly true, but i should get going
now. that patient seemed quite urgent." & she turned
to the receptionist, tapped the wood siding.
so sweet the way she does that. "thank you Mabel
for letting me know. & Ashton, i'll be sure to see you
when i have time. i'm told the wait will be a bit."
oh yes, all my symptoms pushed deep,
next to all the tissue. "just relax."   *we are supposed to*
                                                          just relax?
not a thought of that bump. oh wait—

"do you know what's wrong with the person?" i asked Dr.
Reynolds.
the stretcher-person. the dying-person. the urgent-person.
i wished i could be them one day.
she exchanged a look with Mabel before answering.

"i do not know exactly what is wrong with them, no.
but i can assure you that you do not need to worry about that."
another look. "if they need me, be sure to contact
that number." i saw a sticky note with numbers on it
before Mabel slipped it behind the desk & into their area.
that must be Dr. Reynold's direct number.
a direct way for me to reach her in my time of need.

                                              & 'they'

& 'they.'   swoon.

she blurred away. left through the doors as they pulled open,
shut, open. the others in the waiting area
must have given me the stink eye. i could tell
they were all looking at me. jealous of the attention
i had garnered, much like the stretcher-person.

but really, i was alone with the receptionist. licking the film
of my teeth before i asked if we could call that number.

09:51 AM

"the number?" yeah,

"could we call the number? on that. i saw Dr. Reynolds, & well,
pretty obviously heard her as well."

"as i explained earlier, we have several patients ahead of you."

"i know," head jutted out, a slight pain at the base of my neck,

"but we could still call, right?" my hands twisted up,
fingers fanned out, praying for any sort of help. "i mean,
i'm not entirely confident that we are safe. we could ask for an
update."

"no, i'm sorry Mr.— Ashton. what do you mean by 'safe'?"
another person entered the waiting room. maybe i should return
to my seat. the person hovered behind me, anticipating
my exit so they could check in. their breath a hot rod
against the nape of my neck. actually kind of soothing
for the pain … maybe i should ask to take the number.

their breath expanded hotter. what does this person look like?
i turned around, eyes flashed over the body, enrapt.
they could easily kick my ass & i didn't want any broken bones
on top of the … the bump. but then again, maybe
that would make the bump less … serious.

imagining how brittle my femur would be if held by
such a fist & then broken, shattered & how in agony
i would be, on the floor, rolling in my defeat.
a thing of beauty.

"please return to your seat. i promise
we are working as fast as we can." they said,
when i stepped aside. their smile was not as nice.
not as coddling. it didn't give me the safe feeling.

like gnats, more nurses emerged from various doors,
various rooms & proceeded to the ICU.

their faces stone worried. what could be happening
with that person?

or,   maybe   with me?
are   they   preparing?

all of it an effort to prepare for me. get the ICU rooms
sterile for my bloated death. stomach glutted by eggs
from that damn bump. an insect. a prolixed ending.
ballooning until   *pop.*

i wiped down the seat again. set my ass down first
then keep my legs lifted, crossed as to avoid
touching the floor any longer. the person across from me,

now, read a magazine. Reader's Digest.
i have been having digestive problems.
maybe i should bring that up whenever i am seen.

10:35 AM

i thought i should mention how unsafe it started to feel.
you see the last half hour, more & more staff entered
& exited the ICU. like it must be most of them by that point.
the whole damn hospital taking care of that patient.

the shivers it sent over my legs, slipped between the fabric
& me. but it really started to get weird when they took
another patient back.

the tiny bristles all over my body flocked straight. that's when—
"how long have you been here,
if you don't mind me asking?" the person in the seat
across me, the one with the magazine. their face very sleek,
feminine. lavish red nails. fake, but nice.
it's like i didn't quite hear them immediately. my mind lagged.
"just wondering …"

"oh, i think for an hour or two, maybe."

"that's not so bad."

"no, once, a couple years ago i waited for five hours,
then another time, i don't remember when,
but recently, i waited for like six, then a few times
for an hour or so, few three, few fours."

"sounds like you're here often. have a room set aside?"
little smirk, lips pulled towards dimples. "i really don't mean
to pry but do you have a serious … um, illness?"

"no," well, let me rephrase that.
"well, let me rephrase that, i don't know. do you?"

are … you?

i had never seen them before but i don't pay attention
to the other people. not here, why would i? i'm here for a reason
& unless it's Dr. Reynolds, everyone else is just static.
peripheral fuzz.

are you seriously ill?

i realized that this entire time i hadn't been wearing my mask.
something i adopted years ago. early high school.
cold & flu season. it gave, if even placebo, a sense of protection.

neither did they, of course. i ran my hand over my chest,
made sure no spores had built up within my lungs.
tapped the sternum, internal clearing of the throat.
like i could sense anything with just my touch.
felt no misshapen growing around the bronchi.

"i'm not sure. my throat seriously hurts."

"oh, that's it."

"that's," they laughed, "it?"

i didn't mean to offend them. i know my problems
are not more serious, but a sore throat? even i know that
she could have slept that off. gargled salt water, sure.

but they went back to the magazine.
i'm not good at conversing. small talk, weather, whatever.
i like coming in & talking with the doctors.

they talk business.
& the …

the security guards, what were they doing? two of 'em
at Mabel's desk, all talking. i'd never seen them so,
so visible. i couldn't tell what anyone was saying.
they kept looking back & forth, ICU, front doors, ICU, the seating
area.

i did hear someone talking to me again but what were they saying?

no, what was happening over there. another guard.
exactly how many did they have on shift right then?
a secondary wave of gnats.

"i'm sorry, what did you say?" i asked.

"aren't
                              you frightened

                                                            &
                                                            w
                                                            o
                                                            r
                                                            r
                                                            i
                                                            e
                                                            d
                                                            ?

10:46 AM

why would i be worried? then the front desk phone rang.
the security guard leaned over the desk as Mabel answered.
i couldn't hear what they were saying. why would i
be able to hear what they were saying?

why would you
be frightened?
worried?

i heard affirmations. a mother & their child
in a few rows over, some else got up. another security guard—

ever think about how you could die
from a brain hemorrhage
at any moment
& just die?

—made their way to the front entrance.
where i entered. where anyone normally enters.

ever think about that fish
that swims up the urethra?

put their hands on the pad near the auto-lock.
pushed a few buttons. then pulled open & slipped through
before making a station on the other side of the glass.

you could break your neck
if a scarf gets caught in
your steering wheel.

no, no, no, i don't think about those things,
but i was then. so, i glanced around.

look.

look. why was nobody freaking out? i wanted to freak out
but nobody else moved. all inert mannequins.

what is happening?

Mabel set down the phone, speaker to the desk.
the security guard walked away

what is happening?

back to their office … security room … camera station.
i let my feet hit the floor then stood up.

what is happening?

i'm not sure. i started towards

what is happening?

the front desk when that person stopped me.

what is happening?

hand tugging on my tee.

"aren't you worried?"

"well,

       yes

          now

             i

                a

             m."

10:48 AM

the   hospital

is   supposed

to   make   you feel   safe.

10:49 AM

blink.

the eyelid muscles shuttering.
not working correctly. you could say i developed a tic.
pressure pointed slack on the forehead.

i blinked a watery seed as my vision buffered back into focus.
eyes beat on a stall. an attempt
to reconcile some type of fluid. the room stiffened with tension.
felt like something big was about to happen.

what

is

happening?

like a chain had been tightened over the door handles.
a bar between the door handles. sweat pooled
in the minuscular creases of my forehead.
those little waterways. no way out.

        i blinked.
no way in.
                  i blinked.
were they locking us in? what was happening?
back to the bathroom. another visit.   blink.
drain myself of tension.

          i blinked.

body quivered as i zipped up my pants. palms raw
after the scrubbing. palms red when the water leaves them.

drying.

drying.

only without the r.

as i left, i flicked the light source down but it turned on.
a bright flash popped behind me. overwhelming.

a trigger.

guess the lights had been off. stepped out.
a man knocked on the glass. outside the building.
those wall-sized windows. face covered in blood.

i blinked.

security guard's back to me. standing outside
the entrance. arms crossed. did they not see the blood-person?
where did the magazine-person go?

empty seat.

no

magazine.

i felt my hands vanishing into my sleeves. fabric
folding over itself in bunches. Mabel over there dialing the phone,
looking over to the front door, mouth moving quickly,
quicker, think   quicker.

dialing, talking,
        dialing,   talking.

the window more plasma than glass. not a single movement
from anyone inside the building. as the person followed my sleeves'
lead
& crumpled to the ground all entangled. cruor mere under them.
the other patients continued on as if nothing happened.

dialing, talking,
                    dialing …

                    talking.

was i seeing things? no one had come from the ICU
in what seemed like
forever.

                                  for-
        ever.

10:50 AM

forever until i heard the crackle over the intercom.
     "attention patients of South Regional Hospital,
      due to unforeseen circumstances,
      the campus will be placed in a routine lockdown
      effectively immediately.

     "patients who are currently receiving, or awaiting care
      inside
      our Emergency Rooms will be safely assisted in a timely
      manner.

     "administration will provide additional information as soon
      as possible.
      the hospital is working to ensure the safety of staff
      & patients while the lockdown is underway.
      please know your safety is our
      number one priority."

a routine lockdown?

                         hah.

i had to laugh. what about a lockdown could be routine?
what about a lockdown could be real?

it couldn't be real, could it? a buzz from the seating area,
like the clouds outside finally broke the levee & stormed
the front desk. the shouting, the fear. yes,   *a commotion.*
       finally. fi-   nally.

10:51 AM

the commotion lasted all of a few seconds before it turned
                    into   panic.

"what do you mean by lockdown?"
                    "safe?"
"are we okay?"
                    "unforeseen circumstances?"
                    "safe?"
                                                    "what
                                        happened?"
            "are we okay?"
                                            "i need to
                            see a doctor now!"
                "what happened?"
                                                "lockd
                                    own?"
            "safe?"
                                            "is there a
                                    gunman?"
                "a gunman? are we going to be killed?"
                    "are we safe?"
                                            "provide
                                    additional
                                    information now!"
                "are we safe?"
"what happened?"
            "my son is sick!"
"will i be seen?"

"are we okay?"
"s   a   f   e ?"
"are you sure?"
"are we okay?"
"how long is the lockdown?"
"like shit my safety is your priority!"
"lockdown?"
"are we okay?"
"but my daughter hurt her arm. it's broke!"
"we are not safe!"
"should we be quarantined?"

"areyo
usure
arewe
okayw
hatdo
youm
eanloc
kdow
nhowc
anweb
einalo
ckdow
n"

"my daughter!"
"my son!"

Mabel had no answers for any of the questions.
front desk swarmed by all the concerned people.

i wouldn't even have been able to fit in a word
so i just stayed right where i was. & besides, it's not like

i didn't expect that to happen. you should always expect
a lockdown to happen. my mother taught me that.
you never know when something will happen.
the world is unpredictably predictable. or something like that …
wait, the stretcher-person.

yes.

i bet it had something to do with them.
& when i figured that out, it was all good.

well, not good, internally i was having a meltdown
& i still needed to be seen myself, but what if
something is seriously wrong with them?
maybe they had a deadly virus?

we were all exposed. how stupid i felt then
for not wearing my damn mask. everyone here
could be dead within 24 hours.
no.

no?

no, i didn't know that for sure. i needed to remember
my coping skills. let's be skillful here, okay:
breathe.

i sat back down. put my pointer finger
under my nose to feel the air come out.
look at me, yup, skillful.

back at the desk, people seemed to be dispersing.
water down the storm drain. there's a security guard
back behind with Mabel. that yellow embroidered
SECURITY vest. if Dr. Reynolds were here,
she'd tell me what's going on. i know that.
all i could think of is getting that number, calling her, being with her,
being

seen.

then another guard came out & gently suggested
that the rest of the patients return to their seats.
& they did & you could tell the guard had a gun.
the holster, the way they stood.
if there were a gunman, i'm sure they'd be a big help …

we were trapped.

i'm trapped in a hospital of all places.

11:18 AM

of all the places this could happen, i suppose
i felt the safest there, despite everything.
& Dr. Reynolds would still see me, she'd still
examine all that ailed me. that's what they told us, but …

"excuse me, Mabel." i said. she looked stressed.
that real stress. can-tell-stress.

"yes, Mr. Reed?" she's tried to get those pronouns right,
but i can tell it didn't stick & that's when the lights
flashed for the first time. the whole building in its own
                              blink.

my hands shaken dry of their anxious sweat.
"did you see that?"

"i'm sorry, Ashton, if you will please return to your seat,
we are working through patients in the order
of their arrival & seriousness."

"mine is quite serious & now even more so."
you can't tell me that i was the only one
to notice that? the only one to blink as well.

did i even blink?

a nurse pulled in another patient to the examination rooms.
things are moving forward. "thank you," i said,
turning around. i didn't trust anything.

why would i?

& even for a hospital, it was so eerily quiet.
i heard all my body. that sanguine rush,
that heart flex, that small wish of hair next
to my earlobe being batted around by the ceiling fans.

a little too quiet.

gotta agree.
so i cut the silence by heading into the bathroom.
it's my only option for privacy.

as i walked, i counted how many patients were left.
five in total. six with me. the rest had been taken back.
didn't see a single one return, though.

you know.

& with the lockdown, no one else was coming.
i'd be the last one still.

11:23 AM

one last second of the faucet. my hands soaked
& thoroughly rinsed. let the air dryer woosh
the wetness off me. 30 second wait. lifted my head
& there's me in the mirror. i pulled my eyelid down.
the pupil's bottom molding under the light.

fungal claws between the bloodshot vessels.
my body exhaled backwards, nearly slipped
on the sink drippings but caught myself.

what the hell was that?

i squinted back up to see the normal hue.
deep breath.

below that my nose bone, dried skin flaked.
cheeks noticeably canard, flush.
it didn't feel like my face at all,
but nothing was out of the ordinary.

my nose had no bone protrusion, no gaps
where something could enter. i had to be seeing things.
it's not like my eyes were de-
composing. they couldn't be. i only had one thing wrong
with me now.
       i blinked.

more blinking to wash away that sudden itch.
let me check that one thing that is wrong:

                         the bump.

rubbed my hand over the backside, the nape of my neck.
              there.
              that wart.
the bump was still there.

                    blink.

that's odd … as i pulled my finger away,
i felt a jolt. underneath the skin.

then a poke. a push.
i turned my neck & squinted at the mirror to see.

from my skin burst a leg, a tarry black
& bristled appendage,
then another. the searing edge
of a blade peeling flesh.
they writhed for a moment before a sudden gasp of pain
leapt over me as four more legs ruptured the skin.
how undulated they stretched from the flappy hole.

                blink.

i screamed.
the legs twitched in a staccato rhythm.
millions of hairs
covering the tarsus claws.

unfolding, unpacking itself
from the raised hive.
limbs stretching in a quivering eddy.
clawing, scraping
at the tender opening
to pull its abdomen from underneath.

blink.
i swatted. full palm
like a mosquito
caught before its drink.
blink.
but the thumbed, hardened deposit
burgeoned, more red.
distending from the pressure, an insectile body.

i saw the exoskeleton take form.
blink.
skin taut over the shell.   blink.
again, i tried to pull away,
to grasp at the spindly legs—

b
l
i
n
k
.

another swell of pain & crump,
the rostrum crowned.
my skin broached, a rippling sting

like peeling a hangnail.
its eyes darted, shivering in the mirrored reflection.
mouth gaping,
a rotten gear of teeth. the sound.

        blink.

the sound.
an abrasive grinder wearing down bone
in my ear.
louder & louder like it was fining
the cartilage into ivory talc.

         blink.

"this is it."   the
   d y i n g   .

           blink.
i dropped my upper body on the edge of the sink.
tears streamed down my cheeks.

  blink.   before.
  blink.

i glanced one more time.

       blink.
       & nothing.

57

b
l
i
n
k
.

just a small bump. i don't even know
how to explain it.
            it was gone.

11:39 AM

just like that. gone.

you're okay.

i'm okay. breathe. splashed water
on my face. let it wash away my tears.
look in the mirror. all fine.

"jesus, feel like i'm going crazy."

naw.

"i should head back before—" the door creaked open.
the handle rasping against the tiled wall.
chattered satin nickel.
"hello?" no answer. must have been

the wind.

i popped my head out of the restroom. the lobby
seemed normal, if quiet. it appeared that most
of the other patients had been taken back by then.
swallowed. up by the front desk, Mabel & someone else.
they were dressed much nicer than anyone there.

those ashy eyes, poplar permanence, straight tall
& anemic, a hub for a particular resonance of stuffiness.
hard shoulders, petaled by a crisp suit.
authentically fancy, well-off. the opposite of me.
no microbursts of jitteriness in their hands
as they command the room, motion out each scenario,
two fingers rigid aim. jaw etched stone, wooded goatee.
maintained but natural. all something i could never be.
a man's man.

i made my way back to where i had been sitting
until i noticed that everyone was staring at me.

dozens, hundreds of eyes. pried pupils. the security guard even,
outside the building, their face pressed on the glass.
smudging the hazel of their irises.

i chuckled, that nervous kind of laugh. you know the kind.
where you stumbled into a room with a cult performing
a ritual sacrifice. so i broke the tension:

11:45 AM

well, i didn't break the tension. really,
i just overheard the end of their conversation & had to interject.

"yes, sir," Mabel said.

"& once he," the fancy person said, clearly, unfortunately
talking about me. "gets through the examination process,
we'll escort the rest of the staff to the quarantine area."
there's the word: quarantine. i knew it.
i   knew   it.
we knew it!
wait, did we?

like some infectious disease. me, a petri dish.
"could we have someone take him back immediately?"

"Mr. Reed only sees Dr. Reynolds."

"well, that won't do."

"is she still occupied?"

i hoped   Dr. Reynolds
          was   okay.

"she is, we don't have the capacity for him to wait for her to finish
up, either."

"then, i'll see which other doctor can see Mr. Reed." &, you see,
this is when   i interjected.
i had been creeping my way closer the whole time. inching
from chair to chair then sprung to my feet.

"should i be concerned? i know i heard you mention quarantine
& i'm wondering if i'm in any kind of serious danger or
ifyouthinkthatishouldbeconcerned."

the words billowed from my throat. all strung together.
i couldn't speak any quicker if i wanted to. the fancy-person
looked me over. eyed from my hair to the slight patter
under the surface of my shoes. the kind of look when someone
doesn't even consider the other person a person.
looking over an animal, a caged creature at the zoo.
behind bars, behind evolutionarily.

my eyes wandered away from them towards Mabel,
who smiled. their best impersonation.

"Ashton, thank you for your concern, but we are all be fine.
this is simply a routine lockdown." a phrase, a metered saying
to calm someone down.

the fancy-person butted in. "it's nothing to worry about.
as Mabel stated, your safety is our highest priority,"
pointer finger daggered at me, "& due to that,
you may have to see a different doctor who is available."

then a sound haunted the lobby. a shrill gasping,
gargled, phlegmy.

& it kept going, growing

    louder   & louder
from inside the ICU.

11:48 AM

they both sprinted towards the sound &, for some otherworldly
reason,
so
did
i.

i'm not really sure why i followed. why would i go towards
the danger? what was this inclination in me to swallow danger?

it's like my mind wraps around something &, like a tentacle,
doesn't let it go. the doors torched open behind the brunt
of the fancy-person's shoulders. it probably felt cool, right?

they are cool.

once inside, everything looked exactly the same
as the rest of the hospital. except for a person— a nurse—
slumped over, back against the hallway wall.

i swear: like a mouth puffed, cigarette ashed out between teeth.
smoke crashed from further down, licking along the right angles.
all crispy black & reeked like my father.

but Mabel & the fancy-person must have been too focused
on the nurse to notice when i pointed, finger cocked past them,

& the lights flickered. one by one, blinking down
the ceiling tiles, waxen fluorescents grayed with a shatter.

my throat tightened, SCM muscles bulging against skin,
cramping; a shackle of pain. hands cupped, pinky against
the jawbone, palms praying to stop the spasm.

i'm   not   even sure
why i   followed them.

1?:50 AM

it started to make less & less sense why i followed.
urged by something inside me to seek out
that which could pain me.

all the pressure in an attempt to stop the forming
of a new obsession.
then the nurse's throat ruptured; a cough blurted out.
an echo. & all my worry drifted towards them.

the way their mask's straps tugged behind the ears,
forcing a little redness to appear. & that's when i realized
i was really there.
this wasn't some dream, some hallucination.

                    i

                 promise.

"excuse me, Ashton but you really can't be back here.
I'm sorry i should have—"

"seriously, get him the hell out of here. what the hell is this?
come on now." the fancy-person snapped.
their voice didn't offer any sort of reassurance &
they didn't look at me. people don't often see me.
people look past me. i look past me, too.
the smoke continued to curl towards us & like magic,
one by one, the lights came back on.

& Dr. Reynolds emerged. & then Mabel said:
"here, Ashton, let me walk you to the lobby.
it's not safe for you to be back here—"

"thank you, we can't have any more issues today." the fancy-person
replied,
hand waving over Dr. Reynolds.

"i—i'm sorry, i don't mean to be a hassle, but if something bad
has happened," i couldn't take my eyes off the nurse.
their face, those mask straps indenting.
"i think it's within my rights to know that … well,
a lockdown is, you know, something serious
& if something serious has happened … lookatthenurse!
you can tell. it's not just me."

"Ashton, please, this is no place for you." her voice, Dr. Reynolds,
was all reassurance. wrapped in the kind of hands
that never let you go. & just for me. & just in that moment.
when she tells me it's not safe. i listen.
"we have everything under control. Jackie is simply exhausted."
Dr. Reynolds kneeled at the nurse's side, hand backsided
against their temple.

"i do not care about whether or not you explain
to this kid why he can't be back here.
just get rid of him before i contact security."

him …

him …

i wish they would stop saying that. an uncomfortable tingle
over my arms & shoulders. a pinching fiery nip.

Dr. Reynold stopped them before they said anything further. "Mr.
Padlo,
i'll take Ashton back."

"so is it like—" i looked over into Dr. Reynold's eyes, mine half-
crescents,
dipped in some type of fear, but the greenness of hers looked like
a field.
empty & solemn. like not a blade of grass was touched.
nothing out of the ordinary. "a virus? or microscopic flesh-eating
prions? or parasites?"

"what?" uttered the fancy-person.

w   *hat?*
w   *h*   *at?*
w   *h*   *a*   *t?*

disbelief. upper lip curled on one side.
then they adjusted their tie while standing up.
finger grease visible on the smooth fabric.

Jackie, the nurse, hadn't coughed since the beginning,
so i'm not sure if something was seriously wrong with her.
maybe they could look at her after they take care of me.

"nothing like that," Dr. Reynolds came & placed her hand
on my shoulder. the glove sticking to my shirt.
"nothing of the sort. this happens but please, let's return to the
lobby."

"oh, so it's like …

a conspiracy

a conspiracy thing?

they're hiding something

like are we hiding something?"

"ok! that's fucking enough! do we seriously
have a random patient spreading rumors
about some conspiracy. we are not hiding anything,
& yet both of you are doing nothing
to remove him." such a grated tone.
i never really felt so threatened. from something so outside
my body, but the way they hovered,
approached "he leaves now or i'm banning him from the premise.
we do not have the manpower to handle this kind of shit. okay?
do you understand? he's your problem now Dr. Reynolds,
so get rid of him."

"them." getting between the two of us.

"excuse me, who them?"

"Mr. Padlo, Ashton here is one of our
regular patients. so i feel like we need to be …"

"&?"

"their pronouns are they & them."

"we are a hospital. we do not have regular patients."
Mr. Padlo's fingers were formed in an ok sign,
thumb & finger a circle, flared at the rest of the fingers,
like a fan of terrible spikes. "we have first timers & dead bodies.
& last time i checked this guy doesn't look all that dead."

the uncomfortable feeling continued.

"i was just informing you of their pronouns."

~   ~   *thank*   *you*   ~   ~

i couldn't contain my excitement. she was
defending me. "oh, my gosh, thank you!" though,
dashed so quickly.

"Dr. Reynolds if you continue with this insubordination,
then you'll both be removed."

11:56 AM

oh, what i'd do to go anywhere with Dr. Reynolds.
if only i could go with her wherever.

how safe that must feel. to be encapsulated in her warmth.
but i know that's not how the real world works.

right?

               ...

i apologized for the hassle again.
& the nurse on the ground,
i swear, when their eyes flashed up at me,
   they were onyx.
no iris, cornea, just all black hole.
but by the time
i could take a second look
i had exited that hallway.

back in the lobby, the quiet really took over.
i could hear the gentle stream of my vessels,
the ache within my TMJ, that little shiver
down the back of my legs when i planted
my feet fully on the carpet.

right behind me, the caboose to my train.
Dr. Reynolds came. her face pallid,
shaved down of personality.

a blankness. she walked over to the front desk,
grabbed the phone, dialed & picked it up.
after a brief moment, she began to talk.
asking another nurse to come out.
or something like that.

there's just a couple other people left in the lobby
with us. a child & their parent. & they, too,
look like they have no clue what was happening.
& exactly. neither did i. i don't think anyone did.

how could you? how could anyone?
it'll probably sounds like nonsense as i'm telling it.

sitting down, i looked at my hand.
a little tremble. like a cyst
about to be breached by hydatids.
an unwelcome tremor.

but it didn't matter. Dr. Reynolds walked over
to me. her face a little flusher, cherry.

i was being seen now. finally,
s   e   e   n.

she kneeled down in front of me, my eyes quickly shot
to the empty chairs all around. do you see what i mean?
how much she cares for me. to kneel.

"so, i'm just letting you know that one of my nurses
will come to take you back in a few minutes,

& we'll proceed from there.
i know this must be terrifying for you
& i do apologize for Mr. Padlo's rhetoric.
it's quite stressful, his job. but, please,
i am asking very nicely,
stay in the lobby & do not go wandering off."

"if you say so, Dr. Reynolds."

"thank you for understanding. just stay in your seat
until you are called back. i— promise— you are fine."

"i'm fine?" & she nodded. a smile. the way
her dimples buttoned. & then she left.

& i was alone again.

another nurse entered & took back
the remaining people. that child & their parent.
so, now, truly i was alone. not a single other soul around me.

even the guard was missing from their spot outside
the front door. some lockdown.
i walked over, tugged
on the handles, waved my hand over
the automatic door pad,
then turned around.

nothing budged. energy sapped. trapped in here.
& something awful was happening in the ICU.
i stared at the emergency sign over the doorway.

12:04 ?M

& the sign stared back. eyes coated in that orange-
bordered deadness. i can't tell you how long i stood there,
hands tucked in my pant pockets. absent-minded,
just thinking of everything that had happened.

a freakin' lockdown, you know?

like, didn't think that i would be there.
& i just wanted some help. didn't i deserve some help too?

instead, i'm tossed in the waste bin with the rest of the garbage.
felt just like garbage. i'm garbage & maybe i deserved it.

interesting …

to finally work up the courage to seek help,
once more, & to end up trapped, helpless.

you're probably right.
very helpless.

my mind continued to swirl. toilet water. a waste.

how isolating this must feel.

how isolating it felt. no matter where i ended up going;
i'm lonely in this nightmare. i never felt more alone.

more alone

m o r e

a l   o   n   e a l   o   n   e al   o ne
         alon   *e a lone al o   ne*

                                        a   l   o
                                           n   e

a   l   o   n   e

              a   l   o   n   e
                             a   l   o   n

                                   e

                             a   l   o   n   e
                   a   l   o   n   e

a   l

              o   n   e
                                   a   l

                                        o

                                        n

                                        e

                             a

                   l

                        o

                                        n e

                        a

luna rey hall

                                                        l

                                              o

                        n
                                                              e

                        a

                  l

                                              o

                              n

              e
                                                                          a

                                              l

                  o

                              n

        e

        a

                                              l

                  o

                                        n

e

a

l

o

n

e

.

i think my mind started to slip out
of my ears, my nose,
like so much snot, fluid excreted
from my worthless brain.

my chest tightened. crowbar
bending my ribcage.
each individual rib wrung out.
poking through the skin,
a warped sharpness. a fist of air
or anxiety or that sweet,
sweet impending death feeling
that rattles your blood.
my body never knowing whether
to flight or to fight.

but that's when i saw the nurse.
& i guess i had been sitting back down
by this point because
they told me to stand up
& follow them.

12:25 PM

& they did me up like they do a patient. i mean i know
i was the patient, but they did me up like one anyway.
made me feel all real. the whole patient routine.

sat down in the chair next to the desk, the closest one.
pulled up my sleeve. tugged it high into the armpit.

they told me to cough, show off the strength of my lungs.
but no matter how hard i focused on each alveoli,
those inflorescent little buds, those brachial tubes,
thick branches & rain jacket pleura,
the way my diaphragm flexed, the whole Northern Red Oak
of my chest, i couldn't stop thinking about being alone.

even with them right there next to me.
whispering in stuttered puffs & squeezing
how pressured my blood feels.

then they asked me all the questions
but i just wanted to ask my questions.

they're just going through the motions.
a tabled list. a mockery of my pain.
it's like she's acting as if nothing, at all, had happened.

temperature tongue. 98.7. like this is a normal Thursday
& for them, it might have been. confirmed my medical history.

but look, that person, the stretcher-person,
something was boiling within them

& it seeped into the rest of us.

"so, do you have any concerns i should pass on, outside
of what you wrote down on your form?" not even taking a second
to look up from the clipboard.

"any other concerns?"

you best believe that i had an abundance of other concerns
but wait, what kind of concerns did i put down in the first place?

"i'm … um, what did i write down?"

the way they looked at me. a brown abyss for a moment
before they turned the acting back on. "i believe you said
you had a nodule on your neck, is that true?"

"there's certainly some truth to that." the truth was
i didn't remember. my hand ran along my neck.

i tried to feel every abnormality but were there any?

12:?4 PM

"there isn't anything abnormal about the lump, to me.
it looks like a pimple, maybe a bug bite."

that was a first glimpse.

"but it could be something worse, right?"

"let's hope that's not the case," a wink. an act.

"it's hard to find hope when the thing inside you can't be seen
on a PET scan or can't be felt when you open me up
& fish around my organs or tasted like some moldy grain on
bread.
it's just there, when i close my eyes.
& no one can close their eyes to be there with me."
they pushed back the chair. a screeched wheel
& got up, tapped their clipboard.

"i understand but if that's all, then you should be fine
but i'll be sure to mention it to Dr. Reynolds when she ha—"

& that's when an alarm went off.

the blaring, whistle kind.

gray & white flickered under the door trim.
now i feel i have to say that i promise
this alarm was not in my head.

no matter how much you think it may have been.
it was an actual alarm. i promise: not in my head.

an actual one-hundred percent real alarm. i know this
because even the nurse took note.
eyes perked at the sound,
the direction of the door, then i saw their eyebrows cock
before taking a step closer to the sound.

i wanted to move too, but i couldn't get my body to do
what my brain was telling it to. just a lump in the chair,
trapped in the room, trapped in the hospital, trapped in my mind.

"please, Ashton, if you could please stay right where you are.
we won't be able to help if you leave this room, understand?
please   stay
          here."

& like that, they left. momentary broken solitude returned.
the door heaved to its rest. sighed.

i felt handed around at that point.
given from one doctor to the next.
all i wanted was to find Dr. Reynolds
& be with her. maybe i could have found her
before she found me in this room.
but i was told to stay. stay put.
stay stiff as a gargoyle. stay.
          stay.   *stay.*   *stay.*
stay. it's always stay.

the alarm kept roaring, though it appeared
that the flashing had stopped.
my ears became accustomed
to the sound. add that to the auditory issues.
another tinnitus. it ripped through the hospital,
swallowed everything in its panic.

then it waned.   &
came back.   stronger.

i searched for anything to hold onto
as my heart began
to drum against my skin.
the ugly, greenish, squiggle
patterned fabric on the arms of the chair
looked good enough. fingers dug, sharp edges
of bitten nails slipping in the fabric's cheap softness.

XX:XX XX

my mind drifted back to a year ago. a better time
when i was actually able to have an appointment
with Dr. Reynolds. i can't remember why
i went to the ER that day.

i had a reason but it escapes me.
every fear is so distant now.
slowed by depressive ichor.

i laid back on the medical bed, stomach exposed.
Dr. Reynold's hands testing pressure points near my hips.

"does this hurt when …" two fingers tight against each other
then tight against me. "… i do this?"

i squinted, hoping to be validated by her questioning,
but her hands were indolent. like the rest of my body
decided it would feel nothing when i arrived.
it wanted to shame me for responding to its pestilence with hope.

"no, it doesn't hurt."

"well, that's good," she pulled back & motioned for me to sit up.
"i'm not finding anything out of the ordinary, really."

"but something is wrong."

"i understand, we'll do some bloodwork, a urine test,
but i think this may be a cause of your anxiety.
as i explained last time, your mind can make you feel real pain."

"it doesn't feel like anxiety." & she unskinned her gloves.

"i understand. keep working with the rest of your care team.
i've seen improvements since you started therapy."

"i don't think so. my body is a disaster. it's always lying."

"actually, i think, maybe, you need to start trusting in this body of
yours,"
her left hand over mine, the sincerity of her belief in me.
"if you did, you might not be so scared of it."

12:37 PM

then the fabric began to rip
& as it did, the door creaked open wide.

i shiftily looked around to see if there was a breeze,
if the nurse had returned to open it but no,
just the emptiness of the hallway stared inside
the examination room. checking over my body
to make sure i wasn't dreaming, you know,
the usual:

squeeze the cheek, pinch the forearm,
give yourself a flick.
but i was awake. i swear. & what's worse?
the alarm dissipated
as soon as the door opened.

then a washing silence.

the fluorescents dimmed.

i released my sweaty hands
from the chair, stood up, legs all doe.
all fluid & shake. newborn & frightened.

& tipped over to the door.

why?

well, something opened the door?
doors don't just move on their own,
right?

why not?

i peeked my head out, leered down the hallway
to the left
then as i craned my neck
to other direction.
i heard a noise.

a
wet
clomp.

12:43 PM

clomped into a stomp. louder in my ears.
i could hear every distinct feature
of the noise. the moist pressing, the force, the—

at first, i thought it was a hoof puncturing the cheap hospital tile
with its steel crescent moon.

but the more i listened,
i knew it had to be human.

but it sounded so … not.

a dragging, a hollowness
to the breathing that followed, a bitter pulsing.

you're waiting for it?

even with the tiny chatter
of the broken linoleum, my head wouldn't move.
i couldn't comprehend the thought of looking the other way.

i had to see, for myself, what thing
could be making such a noise.

my chest sprung with an anxious cough.
a thumping of the heart that made
those ribs of mine into worn piano keys.   *still looking?*
& the sound got louder. a closeness.   *bold.*

more dragging. more clopping,
thudding & then a clonk against the wall.
like a person had been shoved.

was the nurse okay?

could they have been injured? was something worse happening
worse?
i, uh, don't know? there could have been.
like i said, maybe,
         an airborne virus.
then the lights waned further dim. almost in line with my racing
heart.
look.

my eyes tracked the shadow bending around the corner.
a person.   at the end of the hallway.
     naked.
well … naked, yes, but in the sense that they had
        no   skin.

all of it excoriated from the vessel. a mix of bones
& muscles & veins & garish, vibrating involuntary knots.

it was almost beautiful the way
i could see the ribs behind a thin flesh sheet.
eyes were deep maroon. pulsing yellowed veins
seeped rancid vapors into the air.
its left leg broken, behind it, knee barely holding on
to the wheelbarrow of its stripped bones.

the hallway practically caved around the person.

they must have been hurt. in such a visible way too.
no matter how you looked at them
shambling towards me, you saw the disease pocking
their entire existence.

how lovely it must be to be hurting in such a way.
such a visible, tangible pain.

tumors all over its hunched back. decay
followed it the closer it crept to the room. dumbfounded.
both our mouths hanging, theirs
edged by thin sinews of rind.

& the approach; no emotion.

alert, if anything. alert to my presence.
the tingling numbness
that washed over my fingertips.   *move.*

as if this opportunity would ever happen again.
& it trudged closer, each step bending the flooring
with its rotten soles.

next step: bent. next step: broke.

                                                    Ashton, move!
but i couldn't. my body wouldn't. i just
stared it down. flakes of tile molting in the air.

ashen ceramics.   blink.

nearly so close. i could have reached out.
the stench of its flesh swarming
my nostrils & in that reel of retch—

b   l   i   n   k

—i pulled my body back into the examining room.
slammed the door shut & scrambled,
tripped over the second chair,
to find something to block off the door with.

12:4? PM

what could stop that ~thing~?

it's a damn, full grown ma— monster,
something my father wanted me to be. obviously,
wasted away by its dying. something i wanted to be.

how could something be walking in such a condition?
adrenaline? that gives people superhuman strength, right?

right.

so, what could stop a pumped up bacteria of a person?

the exam table?

plug the door trim with a bundle of fitted sheets?

those armless chairs?

under the door handle? the biohazardous trash can?

what? give it more?

there was no lock. stench poured under the thin space
beneath the door. i gagged. reminiscent of when
i would pull out tonsil stones. a mixture of debris wafting up
the back of my throat & the stinging from paring
the skin flaps to get at them.

tasted like a sunbaked carcass all over my tongue.
warm flesh rotted, dripped over my taste buds.
& now my mind was solely trying to fixate on my tonsils;
how similar the smell. but what could i do?

covered my mouth & the bottom of my nose
with my hand, i glanced around the room, then pushed
my back against the door.

what of the nurse?

they must be dead. must be. there's no way
they could have gotten away from that thing …

& what was that thing?

wait …
is
that
the
person
from
the
emergency
room?

the quarantined person. stretcher-person.
the-reason-behind-all-of-this person.
my mind speared the idea, tasting it & swallowing.
the reason we— i was trapped.

a stinging sensation rippled
over my forehead. shocking little pain.
little as in surface area.
not as in the depth of its power.

not now.

outside the door, i heard the footsteps
chewing heavier against the tile.

it had seen me. that disease-ridden
skin bag saw me.
& it could be inches from me.   *& it saw you.*
it saw me. with those
melted chocolate eyes. brown paste.

& that's when i heard a stumbling.
weight thundered onto the floor,
a full flop & smash. right outside the door.

heart ruptured at my skin. down,
at my waist, my finger twirled the fabric
of my shirt into a tight knot, cutting off
circulation to my pointer
& middle fingers & i kept tightening.

a vice. a serpent of my own making.
then a gnawing at the doorknob.
        a   jitter.
the cheap metal rabbled against itself.

                                        this is it, isn't it?
                                        all you've been fearing.

was that what i feared?
it didn't feel right.

too dramatic. too outside myself.

the handle went into a frenzy, a convulsion while i pinned myself

to the door. i couldn't let it in. i wouldn't.
fight-or-flight. auto-pilot. no longer me.

it felt like the hinge would pull off. a massive spasm.
my back seizing & shivering with the last of its strength
before the whole of the door stilled.

then a silence.

??:58 PM

silence. sweet, silence.
my mouth guzzled air. a cough,
larynx an itchy passage to a floret of asthmatic punches.

my fingers gripped under the door to feel if anything was there.
little flakes of wood bent against my skin.
nothing. not even a shadow.

the silence was beautiful. reminded me of death.
that pre-death. what people must hear
before they slump in on themselves.

i scooted my knees up, wrapped my arms around them. fetal.
along my thigh, a pinkish red rub. a cut.
an opening from my shorts.
feels like something more. a sour, spoiled spring
of something more.

i shot up, examined the rest of me to make sure this was a)
the only spot & b) real.

my breathing heaved.
oh, you noticed it too.
yes.
could be worse, could be skinless.
how a crater can form & reveal all underneath you.
think.

my chest

inf   l   ate-   deflate-

in   flate-defl   ate   -infla   te-defl ate-

inf   late   -defla te-in   flate-

def   late-inf   late-de flate-

infl   ate-defl   ate-inf   late-   de   flate-i

nflate-def   late-inflate-

de   fla   te-inflate   -defl   ate-in   flate   -def

late   -inf   late-

inflatedeflat   einflatedeflatei nflate inflat   edeflatei

nflatedef   lateinflate inflated   flateinflat   ede

flateinflate

inflatedefla   teinflatedeflateinf   late

inflatedefl   ateinfla tedefla teinflate inflate deflateinflate

deflatein   flate

inflatedeflate   inflatedefl   ateinflate

inflated flateinflate   deflatei nflate

inflatedeflateinflated   eflateinflateinflatedeflateinflatede

flateinflate

inflatedeflate   inflatedeflateinflateinflatedefl

ateinflatedeflateinflateinflatedeflateinflatedeflateinflateinflatedefla

teinflatedeflateinflate

def   l   ate-i   nfla   te-defl—

blink.

a rapid panting. nostrils grasped for oxygen.

the wound appeared to flourish. edges blistered
with a black singe. what could be inside?
did the skinless-person … touch me?

would that be good?
finally a something to point to. this red. this pink broken open.
quivering. & my finger pushed into the wound,
foraged through the muscle, all of it submitting to me.
pushed it aside like garbage in the bin.

blink.

submerged to the knuckle now, fingernail
soaking up the little scraps of broken flesh.

a crescent war.

pain rippled across my whole body, but it felt good. well,
not good but satisfying. necessary.

my hand began to shake. tremors
that churned my finger about the wound.

unable to hold itself still any longer.
violently thrashing against what my mind wanted.

body pushed more blood out.
then i hit bone. that hard stop.

blink.

& nothing. just a wound. nothing deeper.
no source. stunned at my failure,
i anxiously tapped on the bone before wincing

as i pulled my finger out, the cavity pulsed
in pain with the air lapping at it.

but it was there. the mouth of a wound.
pink torn chunks.
a blood fluke.
curds between flat,
sliced open strands of muscle.

blink.

let's look at this logically, please.
i was not rotten.
this wound would heal.
i was not dying.
this wound would heal.
i was not bleeding out.
this wound would heal.
i was not noxious or corroded
or feculent, no infections.

a throb through my leg. like burled redwood,
damaged knot.
a bulbous growth roped around itself.
then i blinked.

a scratch. one line, a couple stuttered dots.
a poem of a wound. not even a speckle of blood.

mayhap a fingernail caught my hand
when i ran into the room. but it's not even open.
but i ...

could still be infected.
i was alive. decidedly so.

the room felt calmer. my breathing hyphenated
by a slower heartbeat. one that didn't thump my stomach
into a hungry daze. finger under the nose. the air relaxed.

like i birthed it from my own green branches. swallowed.
& stood up, my feet a bit wobbly
before making it back to the chair.
my eyes worked over the exam room,
then saw the faucet on.

where was that nurse?

the water lapped at the porcelain round.
checked the door, still nothing,
so i reverted back to the sink.

where was Dr. Reynolds?

& this tingle in the back of my throat. the smell.
how i hadn't removed my tonsil stones that day.

01:?4 PM

you should remedy that, Ashton.

the overhead light scratched at my corneas.

anxious, artificial.

& still the faucet drained.

a haunting. but where was the nurse?
should i turn that off? before it overflowed.

okay,   where   was
                                   anyone?
   sho   uld i tur   n that   off?
            before   it o   verflowed.

when w   ould   the   nurs   e retur n? ·
         sh   ould i tu   rn th   at off?
      b   ef   ore   e it o   verflowed.

      w   hen   would the   n   urse re tu   rn?
              sho   uld   i turn   that off?
              be   fore it overflowed.

   sho   uld i tu   rn th   at   off?
         sho   uld   i turn tha   t off?
              wh   ere was a   nyone?

         sho   uld   i turn   that off?
         when wo   uld the n   urse return?

befo   re it ov erflowed.
before   *it overflowed.*
befo   re it ove   rflowed.
before   *it*   *overflowed.*
be   fore it over   flowed.
overf lo   wed
ve   rfl   owed
erflo   wed
rfl   owed
flowed
lo   wed
owed
w   ed
d

                                          blink.

i shook my head to dust off the panic.
i couldn't let a simple faucet deter me
from cleaning out my poor tonsils.

who am i if not a cleaner?
who am i if not a warden of my body?

hah! i laughed to myself.
coupled by stinging coughs of poor air.
pulled myself up from the chair now,
take a step towards the sink.

                             another train of thought,
                                  entirely,
                                    eh?

something else entirely. no more fear outside that door.
another step, peeked at the door. how sturdy it looked.

a shield from the germs. not as beautiful as the hematic doors
elsewhere but still a barrier. protection.

i leaned over the sink. both of the knobs appeared off.
not turned, not touched. unblemished.
i rubbed my thumb along the vertical groove
before attempting to twist it.

can you imagine how many hands this sink has washed?
every dirty fuck & their mother. who knows. the person with no skin,
no health behind their eyes. just cavities of scourge.

& now look at you, about to take care of yourself
while waiting for the doctor. doing their job for them. how kind of you.

the water wouldn't turn off. just a guzzle.
but it wasn't clogging

not overflowing like i had thought. draining down.
properly, perfectly. it wasn't hurting anyone.

so i looked up at the mirror above the sink.
vision locked with my eyes. opened my mouth.
a stress pinch at the side of my lips. wide.
slid my vision down, so i could see inside

my mouth. those tonsils at the back. marrowy mounds.
how unnecessary they are. how puffy.

i reached my hand into my mouth, teeth rubbing
when my finger felt around for a flap of skin.
& in finding it, i peeled it back to reveal a redder underside.

eyes wobbling to stay focused. closely peered
at the shriveled muscle i was attempting to open like a door.

then i pulled back further digging for the stones.

only to find a trickle of blood. a stream widening
as i pulled back the curtain more until a stench
traveled up into my sinuses. i coughed,
hand releasing from my mouth. tears mushroomed
at the corner of my eyelids from the reflex.

then i returned to the well, peeled it back again
& spotted the creamy conglomeration of debris.

like they say: a stone. truly apropos.
by then though, the stream of blood
only overshadowed by the struggle
to keep my throat from expelling me once more.

fished my finger to punch the stone out,
i cocked my head at another angle.
the smell of excess food, plaque, & more filled my nostrils,
pushed against the septum wall. making a home.

then, i nabbed it. suctioned to my fingerprints,
the stone reeled out from its cavern.
behind it a gag. the blood in rivulets,

where it could force its way down the backside of the mouth
tongue covered by the splatter.

mission accomplished.

pulled my hand from my mouth & up to my eye level,
a steady throb of stabbing. millimeter by millimeter
all throughout my mouth. that flap twitching.
the other side primed for its own assault
but when i examined the tonsil stone,
really looked at it, there was something off.

the smell cascaded to my taste buds.
the taste of decay.

& i vomited.

into the sink. mucus, a spattering of blood.
stone flung off to the side. a blood deluge, a spritz of iron.
i couldn't control my body. just a moil of my insides.

& look at the porcelain. swished in the round cusp of its belly.
a green mucus-wrapped gel that wriggled
as its propulsion came to a stop. arrhythmic. throat hoarse now,
i turned to the mirror. how my lips were wrenched
with dryness & little flakes of the contents of my vomit.

but i felt something,
something move.

beneath my eyeline. ogled back down & saw wriggling.
my stomach churned again.

what could have been inside me to make that?

this brown thumb-shaped thing.
    emerged from the mucus.
        wriggled free of the gunk.
            oh.

a

m
a
g
g
o
t
.

i felt the bottom of my feet tingle like when you sense
something crawling on your skin.

strings of fluid spread then snapped, broke off,
as the maggot pulled itself from my spit & tumbled
over the rest of the mess. surely this was no stone.

blink.

it moved just like lava. slow, methodical.

how did it get inside me?
where was it?

i saw nothing inside my tonsils. how?

was it deep? deeper?

eating away at me from the inside?
i couldn't take my eyes off it.

this grub, this rotten devourer.

i had spit it up just like any phlegm.
i had to wonder how many more were inside me?
could these be what caused the bump on my neck?
botfly larvae. an infestation.

was i but a corpse? food?

there was something gentle though,
about watching the maggot squirm.

i created something. i opened my mouth again,
panned my eyes to see inside it & sure enough:

a static'd swarm at the back of my throat.
white noise of myiasis. i gagged. that agitation.

blink.

i felt nothing though. you'd think that i had felt more
than a gagging. their bodies tickled my tonsils.
their bodies grasped for my uvula.
little pincers in my cavities.

undersides rubbed along the plaque.
they all can't be coming from one spot.

my whole throat must be …

& what if i swallowed one?

would my stomach acid dissolve them?
burn them into bile?

it's impossible. mayhap a sensory hallucination.
i've been told …

blink.

widened my mouth again, i peered back inside.
pouring now, maggots, from every aperture. every little slit.
throat choked on masses. hands shook on the lip
of the sink, trying to sturdy myself. stuck in this deep horror.

holes eaten open. dug through. tunneled.
frozen as this buzzsaw of growth swallowed my ears
& then they all crawled back under my flesh.
every last maggot hidden from sight.

& my body sprung backwards.

??:15 PM

& i fell against the nurse's chair, the desk, knocking over
the computer monitor.

a sharp pain against my spine
as i stumbled to my feet
to get away from the mirror.

eyes squinted as the water dripped from the sink's rim.
darkening the cheap carpet.

& what of the maggots?

what maggots?

hand over my nose & mouth,
breath squeezed between the fingers.
nothing inside me felt off.

more off than normal.

my free hand rubbed along the front of my neck.
tiny stubble flicked as it went up & down.

it had to be a dream.

a manifestation of stress.

nothing more, right?

huh.

i approached the sink once more. handle clearly in
an on position. gripped it tight & pushed it off.

where was that nurse? Dr. Reynolds?
were either of them going to come help me?

then i noticed. at the bottom of the brimming sink,
that single maggot still writhed. drowning now. i stared at it.
if all of that were in my head then explain this? explain this.

how?

suddenly all the water soaked away
into the grub's body. & its engorged eyes blinked towards me.

which frightened me, sending my body backwards again.
this time, back hitting the door-handle.
metal groove & the curve of my spine.
jittered. i jumped around, opened the door & escaped.

all for a second, i felt safe.
whatever that sink contained
could not open the door but then
i remember the person.

that skinless bag of muscles
that roamed the hallways.
i glanced up & down; nothing.

lungs swelled with each inflation.
i put my pointer finger to my neck.

counted the beats of my heart.
rapid, for sure.

but there was nothing in the hallway
that could hurt me, right?

maybe if i could just find Dr. Reynolds.

anyone. but preferably
her.

but i had no clue where to start.
i didn't even really know this section of the hospital.

it's looked different somehow.

should i search the whole of this place? what if
everyone was gone?
& it's just me & the skinless-person?

       ...

you're right. the phone number!

she gave it to the receptionist. whatever their name was.
i wish i could remember anything, ever.

if i could find my way back to the lobby
then i could contact Dr. Reynolds.
or find anyone & they could help.
once more up & down.
i don't know why this looked so different.
it's the same sterilized white, amber toned walls.
the same tiled floor, same fixtures & doors
& red laminated paper-arrows that ...

the red arrows, of course!

then that sound in my ears again,
a revving chainsaw sputtering
its teeth on pavement. shrapnel & friction
spitting every which way.

from behind me, in the room.
i needed to leave.

from down the corridor:
a bang, shuffled crash.   *the person.*
in the direction of the arrows. another bang.
how it rattled the hallway.
shook the foundation, my foundation.

i looked the opposite way.

& the sound billowed,
a fire catching underneath my feet
if i didn't go,
before i sprinted away.

0?:2? P?

followed the arrows. they were all over the place.
every turn had more. like they didn't trust a single patient
could find their way out of a banana bag.

THIS WAY TO LOBBY.
follow the makeshift signs:

IF YOU ARE LOST, FOLLOW ME.

you could tell it was one of those situations
where management told the receptionist
to draw up some signs.

gave em' some nice paper & markers, said
"we can laminate it if that'll look better."

each unique in its own way.
but they were my only guide.

& my legs fusilladed as everything blurred.
this happens. tunnel vision. very common,
i'm assured. do i seem
assured? have i ever truly felt assured?

i'm not sure it's possible.
to be assured of anything.
to believe in something,
in someone. an outcome.

i wish i could.
i wish a doctor could tell me i'm fine
& that's that.

i just can't bring myself to feel any better.
maybe this is nature's way of weeding out
people like me.

eventually,
i came upon a set of doors. a plastic window
let me see in. a lobby. i had made it.

the noises came back. banging thunder.
i couldn't escape them. an insect buzzed
away at my ear drum. a saw rattling its last hectic breaths.

but i made it back to the lobby. & in the lobby:
Dr. Reynold's number. i pushed the doors open.

look at how empty it was.

just how i left it or so i thought.

this must have been a side entrance
for doctors or something like that.

i popped out from behind the counter.
swirled around a wall & found
the front desk. bended over the workspace,
i examined all the sticky notes left scattered.

scratch paper slipped across the floor.
where had she put it?

notes stacked on top of notes,
easily peeled off like aged glue.
names, numbers, names, names,
names, dates, times, numbers,
a drawing or two.
"remember to call about John."

John.

could that be the quarantined person?

could be.

shadows flickered in my periphery, unerring.
that tunnel
vision
teared away
just enough
to let in some
distinct forms.

like occlusion adhered apart,
i opened up my eyes
to take in everything.

??:26 PM

i noticed that
       i'm not alone
            in here   either.

across from me in one of the nearer lobby seats:
another person. the skinless-person, skin on.
human, at least.

face shrouded by this half-flicker. claws of light
dragged down their body.

                         the stretcher-person.

clothed now. suit. black, silver-buttoned,
JCPenney-looking tie. not as fancy as Mr. Padlo.

another patient maybe? what was he doing here?
ah, look at me. fuck.

                         how awful of you.

what were they doing here?

the person stared.
pierced right into me. green eyes like algae.

speaking of, where was the receptionist,
the security guards?

& that's when the person shifted in the seat.
hips moved to one side; they pulled out a pistol.
this old Smith & Wesson model. wood handle.

something my father
would have owned.

that whole time they never took their eyes off me.
felt moss growing between my toes, this unease.

i ducked behind the counter. were they here to shoot me?
an active shooter sent this place into quarantine?

not some disease but—
                                        a click.

slamming of ignition, hammer, metal.
twenty seconds went by. more metal grinding.
then another click. i'd heard that before.
they were pulling the trigger. over
& over. click after click.
the chamber must be empty.

i slid my face up, met the countertop
& peered over it
with the top of my head, eyes halved.
the person had the gun
in their mouth. eyes
now drawn down. an emptiness.

saliva oozed from the side of their lips.
almost like praline, congealed
& sticky. a confection of melted flesh.
plopped on their shirt as they kept pulling.

finger rested for a moment,
a second, if that, then another.

like they were practicing suicide.

suddenly, they removed the pistol
from their mouth,
arm flopped to their side,
limp. & their eyes
contacted mine again. this look.
i don't want to ever see that look again.

eyes rusted sunset.
that pre-tornado green.
tree leaf hanging on by a fiber.
& their wrist. that dangling wrist.
a combination of scarred over,
fresh cuts. droplets of blood.

d
r
i
p

d
r
i
p

d
r
i
p

??:2? ?M

onto the carpeted floor. splashes of copper
sponging through the ashy colored nylon.
how the pistol stayed glued
to their palm despite the angle.
wrists trickled over the polished steel.
then this sound. an abrupt wheeze,

the whole of lungs breaking apart.
the person dropped
the pistol to the floor & glared above them
& then i noticed the rope.
sectioned off, knotted, noosed.
free end straight. perfect.

another cough.
a clearing.
vocal cords warming to the air,
warming to me, maybe,
warming up like it were the first time
they functioned in years.

i see you.

were they talking to me?

their voice sounded so
familiar. i couldn't tell from where.
striation after tawdry striation.

these almond-pale scars
from cutting all over their forearms.
yet despite that

they mustered the strength
to lift themselves up,
standing on top of the chair.
forehead nearly leveled

with the noose when the veneer
of their flesh peeled apart.

each of those scars opening
& this echo fulminated
in the lobby's heart.
i see you. i see you.
i see you. i see you.
i see you. i see you.

i see you.

i see you.

i see you.

i see you.

i see you.

i see you.

"you see me?" don't ask me why
i let myself ask.
i felt i needed to talk to them.
& it's not like i was having any luck
with the phone number.
nobody else was there

& they
        saw
                    me.
                            they
            saw
me.

01:?? PM

i see-ee-ee you.

how their wrists warped with indicia up
to the forearm. a continual slit
ushering blood. i don't know how.

an unknown, unseen force pulled out
the scrim of their body, a fine thread undone.

razored & razored. distal tendon split,
violently wriggled
for a second before spooling up
the elbow pit.

a congealed chunk of innards
all bulging, pulsing, oozing out
& then a flex of the muscle to push it away
from the bones. an ulna scraping
with the metal tongue.

you wish this were you …

"i wish that were me? what do you mean?"

killing myself? i'd never once thought—
i'd never once created a plan. that's not my style.
my body was doing a good job on its own.

you wish—

they nestled their head through the noose,
the rope another chin, formerly tensile fibers
sprung like bluestem shoots.

& as hemp strings abraded their cheeks,
i thought it all over.

pigment all but shriveled away. translucent
to the point of seeing the machinations underneath.

it's like everything i'd ever idea'd. well, okay,
no, i said i haven't planned, & while that's true,
it's not not true that i haven't idea'd.

those are very different things.
i know i'm objectively depressive.
clinically so. but subjectively,

i don't want to die.

that's terrifying, i think.
i just know that i'm going to die.

this dread & if that dread
is a normal part of your life,
every day, day in & day out,
Monday after Tuesday after—
well you know, maybe.
but there's a big difference

between knowing you are about to die
& wanting to.

i didn't know if i wanted to.   i just wanted it to end.

& i didn't want the bump to rupture my neck,
to blast apart my muscle
so there's a crater
people can look into &
i don't want my lungs to collapse.
i don't want my heart to stop. i don't want
vision to erode, my teeth, my skin, my—

you get the picture.

but you're so good at dying.   i am.

their neck fully embraced by the rope.
snug so there's a red ring of pressure built up
on either side. a sadness in their eyes.
it reminded me of me. everything about them does.

*if you think you are good at dying. that you
know better. then prove it. for once.*

& they kicked the chair out from under them.
this thud.

what followed was a gargling, a struggle.
legs flailed, clawing to rip the rope away.
to un-do. like they had no clue what it would feel like.

a palpable nattering of fear. but the expression
on their face didn't budge. feeble & pallid.
colorless. etiolated tone sunk lifeless.

& we looked into each other's eyes as they died.

i didn't raise a finger.
it's not like i couldn't have stopped them.

i could have, easily, jumped over the desk,
sprinted over, tugged the gossamer.
i could have saved them. at the very least,
lifted up the chair back & returned their feet.
but i didn't.

                                        i didn't.

we just watched each other.

the both of us in this liminal space between life & death.

& when their body finally came to a stop.
a few twitches. i forced my head down,
eyes roaming the rest of the desk
until a synapse went off & the coloring
of the person's neck, that beet-red ring,
reminded me of the color of the sticky notes
that Dr. Reynolds had in her office.

which lead me to find those burgundy stickies
& sure enough,
i found the note,

the number, "if Ashton ..." but what now?
                    i had to find
                              a phone.

0?:3? ?M

there had to be a phone somewhere on the desk.

in a frenzy, i slapped over a mug, slid
a stack of manilla folders off the edge
then scrambled to filch the phone & its stand.

pulling it with me, i slumped to the floor,
old, spilled coffee tapping down on me.
cord strung taut against my shoulder.

not even giving a second thought
to the person hanging out there. lungs harsh,
i could feel pricks during aspiration.

hurry.

not sure why i'm feeling rushed.
pressed in the numbers then
began to hear rustling out in the lobby.

no door opening, nothing to indicate
someone else entered.

finished with the last number, i picked up the receiver
& held it to my ear. hands quaked.

ring.   ri-ring   ri-ring.
  ri-ring   rin-g   ring

ring,   *ring,*

                                  ring.

ring.   ri-ring   ri-ring.
ring   rin-g   ri-ring

                             r—i—n—g.
                             voicemail, eh?

a crackled voice began its message:

?1:?? ??

"hello. you have reached the office
of Dr. Berenice Reynolds. unfortunately,
both her & her team are unavailable
at the moment. if this is a medical emergency,
please dial 9.1.1. ...—"

if you are Ashton Reed, then please
hang up the phone. you chump.
you are already a lost cause.

"—leave a message
after the tone."

"hi, um, i'm Ashton ...
i was just hoping to get in contact with, um,
well, i am actually already
in the hospital like right now, & i guess,
um, well, i was hoping i could speak
with Dr. Reynolds,
she knows me,
i'm sorry, i don't really need to leave
a message because
you are in here somewhere.
& i'm sorry about saying sorry ..."

the voicemail timer was so short.
between its allotted length & my stammering,
how could i have said anything of substance?

& why didn't she answer?

it rang.

she's here.

her team is here.

did something happen to her? was she okay?

was i okay?

      thud.

how a body would slam to the floor. swinging sound
coming to an end.

i could hear the tiny fibers of rope separating.

if you think
you
are
so
good
at
dying
then
prove
it.

that voice. egging me on.
how would one prove they are good
at dying except by dying.

but there's no reward. no prize at the end.

if you think
you
are
so
good
at
dying
then
prove
it.

hands trembled; phone stand set on the floor.
i brought my body back up
& watched the hanged-person
walk through the hemaPRO doors
on the opposite end of the lobby.

like they wanted me to follow.
like they wanted me to prove it.

i'm not good at dying.

i just was

                    dying.

it wasn't about proving that i'm good at something.
it was about getting people to believe me.

a verifiable disease.

all this hadn't been in my head.
that i'm able to show you something.

pus & blood. shriveled cells. arteries clogged.

something.

??:?? PM

so i followed the hanged-person.
who cares where the nurse was,
where Dr. Reynolds was.
it's not like either of them
would help me at this point.

they would just smile & nod.
like everyone else did.

empty. each passing room, empty.
medical drapes stopped me from peeking in,
as if anyone were still there.

i couldn't find the hanged-person anymore,
were they even real?

i saw them die, didn't i?

"hello! hello!
is anyone out there?"

yet there i was, shouting for someone.

hallway bleak. shattered light fixtures.

        be   lieve
        me.

a moaning from the end of the hallway,
off to the left.

& this is when my mind began to spiral.
everything that had happened.

& nothing to show for it.

my wrists clear of injection marks.
no mouth microbiome
or little hijackers, overnight mutations,
gut flora bacteriophage.

i'm no outbreak.
bloated digesting. hydrocarbon forest floor,
orange emulsion, fruiting cock.

at every turn, i was given a clean slate.

but something was wrong.

& i needed to figure it out.
    &   prove
           it.

i'm not letting everyone think
i was lying. i was not lying. something was wrong ...

something was wrong. something was wrong. something was wrong.
something was wrong. something was wrong. something was wrong.
something was wrong. something was wrong. something was wrong.
something was wrong. something was wrong. something was wrong.
something was wrong. something was wrong. something was wrong.
something was wrong. something was wrong. something was wrong.
something was wrong. something was wrong. something was wrong.
something was wrong. something was wrong. something was wrong.
something was wrong. something was wrong. something was wrong.
something was wrong. something was wrong. something was wrong.
something was wrong. something was wrong. something was wrong.
something was wrong. something was wrong. something was wrong.
something was wrong. something was wrong. something was wrong.
something was wrong. something was wrong. something was wrong.
something was wrong. something was wrong. something was wrong.
something was wrong. something was wrong. something was wrong.
something was wrong. something was wrong. something was wrong.
something was wrong. something was wrong. something was wrong.
something was wrong. something was wrong. something was wrong.
something was wrong. something was wrong. something was wrong.
something was wrong. something was wrong. something was wrong.
something was wrong. something was wrong. something was wrong.
something was wrong. something was wrong. something was wrong.
something was wrong. something was wrong. something was wrong.
something was wrong. something was wrong. something was wrong.
something was wrong. something was wrong. something was wrong.
something was wrong. something was wrong. something was wrong.
something was wrong. something was wrong. something was wrong.
something was wrong. something was wrong. something was wrong.
something was wrong. something was wrong. something was wrong.
something was wrong. something was wrong. something was wrong.
something was wrong. something was wrong. something was wrong.

something

is

wrong.

i'll   make sure   of it.
my death won't be easy to pin down
like a dead monarch on a board.
crispy wings crumbling.
something beautiful & worth quarantining
an entire hospital for.

one of those diseases trapped in ice
for centuries, waiting to be melted
& released. filth praised
for its resilience & pumice shell.

that's when i found the room
at the end of the hall.
this little nook of a corner. with my elbow,
the curtain trundled to a scrunch
against the wall. in the doorframe,
one foot tucked behind me
in case i needed to make a quick escape.

hands at my side, trembling.

0?:?2 ??

the tremble flocked over the rest of my skin.
shivering arm hair. in the middle of the room:
the person. you know, them.

their corpse, i suppose.

they looked dead. a potential future.
the room looked left-in-a-hurry. like everything else.
this peculiar disappearance.

& i stood there. there in front of me was the person
that started the whole thing. tangible blame.

so, hell, i walked forward to the corpse
like it were mine.

blink.   so quiet.
                         blink.

hovered over the body, i examined it.
loss of its personhood.

lips fat like water-soaked caulking, turned black
by the dampness of the skin around it.

i pulled down the drawsheet.
with it, the squeaky wheels of the stretcher swiveled in

& around themselves. i saw the sutures.
rancid, dried-out catgut. already degrading,
flakes peeled like birch.
leathery sacs of pus, seamed-shut pores of ooze.

& how i reached out my palm over the flesh's
lithe existence. its desiccation.
its throbbing coldness against my skin.

what could be inside?
                    could that be me one day?

my eyes scanned down
the rest of the body. jellied-plastic sheen.

                                                    blink.

cauterized even, glue holding the skin;
making sewage. all of it a vibrating mass

                                                    blink.

of other parts. a human conglomeration.
flesh flan.

                                                    blink.

body spattered with bulging, overfilled
balloons. squirming sheets of yellow fluid.

                                                    blink.

the legs tissue-damaged, brown sealant
consistency wracked with needle sized holes

                                                    blink.

& i snapped my head away.

blink.

my hand unconsciously slipped
to the back of my neck, felt the tiny bump.

rubbed my thumb over the skin,
hoping, or not, that something

would burst forth. a proving.

then i noticed this gash on the corpse.

between the lower neck & the armpit.
my head canted. skin serrated over
like ripped paper. if only i could take that from them.

if only i could prove them all wrong.

i bent over the stretcher, stomach pressed
on the metal bar, & really looked inside the wound.

blink.

pale flaxen edges, infected, but the innards
were still this bright red. all caked in blood.

my hand gripped on the bar,
leaning in further.
depth vanishing as my head got closer.

blink.
if i could just scoop it up & show them.
blink.

my mouth inches away.
blink.

that's not very self-preserving of you.

it's not self-preservation.
my whole existence
has been a worrying act
of self-preservation.
& where has that gotten me?

look at me.
i'm bubble-wrapped, scrubbed clean,
a hair trigger away
from a meltdown at any given moment.

no, this isn't for self-preservation.
it's for weaving those real threads of truth.
self-fulfilling prophecy & all that.

the open mouthed throng. letting the body drag
itself into the mud filled with whom knows what.
all an attempt to prove to the others that
I'm what i say i am.

contaminated.

sometimes you need to step up
& do it yourself.

salivating at the gore before i pulled back.
my legs still all doe. barely able to stand.

i looked around the room
then returned to the corpse.

all those little pus sacs blinked across the body.
i could have taken some. i could have
taken it from them.

moved my hand over the wound. all shaky.
i shoved it in. hand entered the lesion.

they looked so peaceful. dead. dreamy.

& look at you.

my fingers pushed around. the insides so wet.
a pool of blood at the end of what i could reach.

peeled my hand from the vector & watched
chunks slip out. dangle on the edge
& my hand flush with the chest's blood.

i turned my palm towards me.
blood ran down my wrist.

was that enough?

blink.
was i infected? does it work like that?   *i don't know.*
blink.

i didn't feel anything. anxiety
jittered my hands but i didn't feel
any infection course through my body.

i snapped them against the air,
flickers of blood spurted on the floor.
i looked over the body once more.
maybe the infection was in the boils.
the sacs. all lined up like raw tobiko.

maybe there.

i pushed back the exposed muscle
of the wound, tucked it under the flaps
of skin then shuffled down
so i was closer to the legs. right in front of me

this translucent dome. you could almost see
the silvery fluid swirling beneath the skin.

like it had its own tide.

i needed to pop it open.

consume it.

?1:44 ??

pinched between my thumb & pointer.
the skin elongated
but didn't pop.

on the other side,
i saw a tray with utensils.

a medical knife, uh, a scalpel.
i reached over the body & snatched it.
fleck of black gunk still stuck to the tip.
i wiped it off
on the side of the drawsheet.   blink.

?1:44:23 ??

holding it over the sac,
then lowered down to the birth of skin.
right on top of the dead collection of cells
that colored the surface area white.

i took a deep breath.
lungs stinging. then pressed the edge down
& slit the abscess.
a squirt. pale liquid. gushing down

the side after the explosion onto my shirt.
a little blood, a little pus.
pulled the scalpel away.

i thought something more would happen.

blink.

?1:44:41 ??

another pustule down the leg. slit that one too.
same thing. the blade covered
in this runny spume of disease.

brought it up to my mouth, my lips parting.
tongue extended
& i licked the dull side.

a startling pungent gout overwhelmed my mouth.
drunkenly tripped all over my taste buds.
i couldn't control myself.

blink.

?1:44:?3 ??

one more uncut sac that i could see.
the largest of them all. this throbbing mass.

painfully red. crusted head.

it opened as easily as the rest though.

spilled more, sodden deflated.
none of it looked different

so i decided not to taste this one.

maybe like a cold sore, more viruses were incubated
in a large one but … i don't know.

maybe my anxiety was taking over.
maybe i was chickening out.
maybe i needed to do something more substantial
to get the rot inside me. i surveyed the body again.

not like i hadn't done that
a hundred times but i had to find another way in.

?1:44:?? ??

that had to be it.

> *what?*

i stepped back up towards the head, tapped their lips
with the scalpel then dropped it on the forehead.

it wasn't much help anymore.
what could i cut that would make a difference?

> *do it. prove it.*

again, i noticed the wound. under me. bobbed my head down,
chin fat collecting in a thick rope.

> *prove it.*

i was not rotten.
i was not dying.
i was not bleeding out.

but i could be.

i rested my palm against their sternum.
stringy chest hairs peeked between my fingers.

dragged my hand down
then thumbed the edge of the wound.

this close, you could really smell the gangrene.
i slipped my thumb inside & hooked it

under a flimsy flap. encyst. wiggled my thumb to the side,
back & forth & worked the meat from its lodging.

it suctioned off from its hold
& flopped into my hand, undulating.

pulled it close to my own wound.
this flabby chunk of a person

i never met before their death.
this intense feeling.

a person in my hand.
a person i had never even spoken to.

does that make it better?
                       blink.
waft of sweet cologne. rubbed down.
barely distinguishable. mixing with the rancid infection.

a sour battering of air.

squeezed flesh inserted into my thigh, though
my wound not big enough. its mouth
too small to consume the rot.

hands quaked trying to force it in.
the bottom squishing against me.
flickers of blood cut out from under.
                             b li nk.

i let it drop. looked over at the person. trailed the thin IV
from their arm to the stand next to them.

the hungry bag sucked in on itself.
bag sucked in on itself.
bag   sucked   in on itself.
        the   bag.
                    the   bag.
                        the   bag.

            blink.

a corpse that did all it could to save the body
& there i was defiling its attempt.

                            blink.

?1:44:58 ??

what

        did

              i

              just

              do

              ?

       b   l
       i   n

                  k

             .

?1:44:5? ??

you would never do this.

my body caught in a deep

                p   a   n   i   c.

s

     h

        a

            k

               e

                   n.

the flesh tumbled out from inside me.
smacked the floor with not so much a thump.

how could i have done this?

it went against everything i'd lived for.
purposely putting myself in danger.

i haven't done anything like this.

i would never. this wasn't me.
i was fucked. i fucked up.

i raced over to the sink. whipped on the faucet,
cupped my hands, allowing a fill,
& poured it down my legs, then into my mouth.

scrambled to pull out some paper towel

from the dispenser. scraped my tongue
against the paper towel.
gagging. coughing up anything i could.

the feeling of a ball of snot
at the back of the throat. tears began
to amass at the edge of my eyelids.
i really fucked up.

i don't know what got over me.

who knows.

i fell to the floor. back against the gray cabinets.
i let myself get caught up.

body in a frenzy. snapped each cabinet door open,
in hopes i'd find something
to clean out my wound, grabbing
each black & brown bottle.

cracked the lids. submerged. full splashing.
covered myself in the solutions.

brackish sting, alcohol singe.
grabbed more, more, more.

bottles flailed empty across the floor.
up & more paper towel. scrubbed,
brown flakes left behind.

enough force to break blood vessels.

i—
i—
i needed help.

how could i undo it?

how can i stop—
the door creaked open.

sliver of light smoothed
across the floor, revealing my shirt
dirtied with a fat ring of warm sweat.

i looked over & saw Dr. Reynolds.

this was all you.

it wasn't me this time.

0?:?4 ??

oh thank god, Ashton. we've been looking for you everywhere.

                                                                we

were

                                                                 so

worried.

"who? me?"

of course!

"i, i did something really bad."looking past her,
the open door shuddered with the brightest of lights.
piercing bleached ooze.

maybe it was all in my head.

it's going to be okay.
it's all going to be okay.
trust me.

                                                                 trust me.

you need to return to the examination room though,
so we can treat your wounds.

                                                                  please,

you can't just be wandering around
the hospital. especially on this side.
we are still in quarantine you know.

we are still in quarantine

you

k

n

o

w.

"i did something really bad.

i am dying."

i understand you are worried. it will all be fine.
here, take my hand.

we don't believe you.

latex palm. i'm used to not being believed.
to be seen as a walking lie.

she had to see the cadaver behind me.
the puddles of peroxide.

had to see how i had infected myself.

right?

follow me.

"thank you."

what?

what else should i have said?

i pulled myself up from the mess i made.
walked around the corpse, hip hitting the edge
of the stretcher as i passed
& peered back one last time.

Dr. Reynolds there, motionless, still.

i can't even see the air entering or leaving her.

let's go examine you. that'll clear everything up.
"but …"
let's go examine you. that'll clear everything up.

                                        this is all what i wanted to hear.
                                               isn't it?

"but …"
you don't sound well.
let me help you.
i assure you.

                                                 hah.

you haven't done anything bad.
& if you have,

                                             i'll be here

with you.

                                               hah.

you don't sound well.

                                             you don't—

i've been looking
everywhere
for you—

                                             sound well.

hah.

sound well—

hah.

we were worried—

hah.

*we were all
worried*

sick.

so,

so

sick.

she made a move towards me.
an effort to calm, an effort to catch,
to detain. something i didn't appreciate
& my arms just acted on their own
as i pushed back. a cough

as the room's curtain discharged
behind my push. she was gone.
a flapping until the curtain stilled.

01:?? PM

gone, she was gone like that.
behind the curtain.

i must have pushed her.

what was wrong with me?

                                                          i am dying.

eased the curtain to the side with my elbow.
the hallway looked different.

a single path. washed in a dusty fluorescent
above a door at the end of the path.

followed it.

i had to get away from that body.

i was dying.

if they found out what i did.
                                        if you found out what you did.
this creaky whisper spun around the inner lobe of my ear.
                                        no one would believe you.
                                           no one believes you.
                                              no one you.
                                                no one.

no

                                                             one.

no   *one.*

                                                             blink.

temple seized by a flash of pain.
shooting along the curvature
of my face. door slammed; open mouth.
my body crumpled in on itself.

blink. i am dying. my entire body caught in this rupture.
this deterioration. an apex of suffering.
my thoughts pulled back curtains
like those operating rooms.

letting me see myself shoving dead meat inside me.

tasting,
licking,
barfing.

the sudden onset of retching.

                                                  b   li
                                              nk.

the door at the end of the hall blinked open.
right alongside me.

i needed help. i had to move forward.
                        blink.

                              b
                              li

                                 nk.

  i was dying.
        i was dying.
              i was dying.
                 i was dying.
                    i am dying.
                       i was dying.
                          i was dying.
                             i was dying.
                                i was
                       dying.
                                       i
                    was
                    dying.

                                          i

                          w

                          a

                          s

                          d
                          y
                          i
                          n
                          g
                          .

the patient routine

161

i

w
a
s

d
y
i
n
g

.

luna rey hall

wasn't i?

??:????? ??? ?????? ? ? ??? ? ? ?

i had a dream once. i woke up on a beach,
the Pacific Ocean,

& i was under this thin layer of sand
enough where you could still see some of my skin

& i began panicking because the tide
was creeping in, little by little,

& my body was in shock, you know that
absolutely frozen kind, because when i looked down
my knees were completely gone.

dissolved, eaten away.

cartilage, kneecap, meniscus, tibia
& femur grinded to a curve.
all that was left was the ligament
on either side. flattened
like ribbons with no wind.

teeth gnawed the circumference,
clearly. nothing but holes now with sand filling
their new guts. those ligaments the only thing
connecting me to the lower part of my legs.

& the tide licks at me

before retreating. i'm trapped.

this beach coffin. something hallowed
my knees away, the ocean
is about to smother me
& all i can think of is that:

i'll have to figure out
how to live with this;
wheelchair education,
shower removal,
clothes on & off, those ADLs,
dependent on others.

body no longer waterproof.
how to walk with prosthetics,
the phantom pain.

it wasn't terrifying that the ocean
was about to consume me,

that i was helpless to escape.
it was terrifying that i might survive

& have to live.

?1:?4 ??

it didn't feel like dying.
that overwhelming sense
of desperation to scrape
onto anything you can hold.

that bright light moniker.
golden beam, tempered steel,
an arch. i shouldered the door open

& stepped inside.

doesn't feel like dying, does it?
how would i have known?
i had never died before. i've told you this before.

but you were right.

it didn't feel like dying.

it's all the more frightening.

my eyes blinked
as i looked around the room.

bookshelves, framed awards & degrees,
mahogany desk, that little thing you can put a pen
into.   *a pen holder.*

such a fancy office.
an office my father would probably have.

an office my father would have wanted
of me. the office of a man.

at that moment, the bump
on the back of my neck stung.
red hot.
my hand against the skin;
a slap & held it.

it's breaching.

b
   r
     e
       a
        c
         h
          i
           n
            g

skin a cocoon for the birth of another.
body a vessel. carapace for death.
ssh. quiet down.
i will not spiral.
the bump is simply a bump.

not now.
you think you did all that
& you'll get away now?

my thumb pressed hard on the mark.
holding the pain in place.

is that it?
you didn't
even listen
to me.
& i'm always here.

breathed. finger under the nose.

always.

i smell an aged, air worn cup of coffee.
hear the faint chirp of medical equipment.
i feel the roughness of my jeans
against my calves, a drip of sweat down
my groin, a drip of sweat bedded in the dimple
of my right cheek, a fan.

a breeze, a breeze, a breeze.

        alw   ays.

logic. logically.

a   lwa
          ys.

blink.

logically: it was a pimple, a scab, an abrasion.

skin ever changes. morphing to fit the environment,
to heal, to restore. i knew this.

        a   lw   ays   s

logically: i had no clue if what i did would cause me any harm.
i don't know what that person had.

not every death can transfer.

        alwa   *ys.*

from touch, my sight, my smell, taste, or simply hearing
the pain of those wasting away. it doesn't work like that.
no maggots. no skinless people.

al   *w*   *a*   *y*

           s.

      blink.

all in my head.
hallucinations. visual. auditory.

                    l
                    a
                    w
                    a
                    s.
                    y

blink.

hallucinations happen all the time
with stress.

w   y
a   a   s.
l

blink.

right?

a—l—w

blink.

a—y—

i can do this.

hey.

be skillful.

—s—

hey!

are

you

listening?

??:1? PM???????

i said 'are you listening, Ashton?'

what?

someone is talking to us.

the pain subsided & i heard a voice.
"i feel like i have to start with
'what the hell are you doing in my office?'"

my eyelids had been sealed tight. thin, plastic
zipped tight. so the voice startled me.
it was, uh, … Mr. Padlo. that voice from earlier.

"this is your office, i'm—"

"that's what i just said, wasn't it?
how'd you even get in here?
this whole area in under lockdown.
weren't you taken back?"

i couldn't do anything but shrug.
the last few hours were a blur,
to use a cliched phrase. then this rush
in my blood, this urge to ask …
one last time. "i did something bad.
i don't think i'm going to make it.
would you help me?"

"oh, no— absolutely, here let me examine you,"
he gestured towards the chair next to his desk.

this brown pleather, ancient thing.
i made my way over & slouched into the seat.
him next to me. this aura of hope.
maybe he's not as bad as i thought.
he'll see if something is wrong with me.

i mean, at this point, any doctor could see what i did
& see the damage. he'll notice too. "you seem to be
in a bit of a panic." his palm against my shoulder.
warm. "which makes sense
since you are wandering around an, supposedly,
inaccessible area for patients.
what were you thinking? do you not read signs?
is that another thing you don't believe in?
signs? reading comprehension?"

his palm shifted its strength to his fingers,
pressing down into my skin. "i could have you escorted out
of the building, but instead, look at me:
willing to ease your anxiety by giving you what you wanted
from the beginning, right?"

"what do you mean?"

"i've seen your records. i understand what you're all about."
nails scratching away the fabric of my shirt.
my shoulders sagged, then bent back to their broad,
relaxed position. "you come here,
once or twice a month … i really didn't believe my staff
when they told me about you,

but here you are. once or twice a month,
like fucking clockwork. seeking validation.
seeking help for an invisible war.
& you may have dragged Dr. Reynolds
into the abyss with you, but i've seen your kind come & go.
you won't keep her on your side for long.
actually, you need people like me.
people in the system," he squinted, rolls of wrinkles
crowed his forehead, "i've been here for a long, long time.
i've worked my way from an intern,
decades ago, all the way up to Director.
so, really, i'm the best type of person to help you.
i have knowledge. experience. morals."
the wrinkles dissipating into his rich, peach skin. "now,"
a pause. he let go of my shoulder & i reactively shot
my own hand to the spot to rub it down with pressure.
an attempt to ease the pain he placed on me.
if there were … any pain there. "i'd love to examine you.
i know things must," he stepped over to a bookcase,
removed a container, opened it,
& pulled a stethoscope out, "have been terrifying.
with the lockdown & everything, so let me help you."

"really?"

he nodded. his chiseled oak face got close to mine.
that hot forestry breath. the mouth of the stethoscope
on my chest now. he gave this awkward smile.
but he was helping me, someone here was helping
& he'll see what i did & how i can fix it.

the sound waves of my heart to his ears.
the no-chill rim of its lips. he listened for a few moments.
i took in the room deeply. every last drop of oxygen.

he stopped.
"that all sounds good."

how?
stop questioning it.

he dropped the ear tips then
wrapped the tubing around the back of his neck,
letting it drape him like a necklace.
"it all sounds good. almost as if nothing is wrong so far,
but i trust you to be honest with me,
so the next thing i'd like to look at,"

another pause,

"take off your pants   & underwear."

??:5? ???????????????

"excuse me?"   *you heard him ...*

i know that you need to look at that stuff
sometimes but ...   oh ...

"i asked you to take off your pants & underwear."

"heard ya'."

"then."

"why?"

"well, i need to see what's in your pants before
i know how to help you, isn't that right?
wouldn't you agree that i would treat a penis
differently from a vagina & vice versa.
would you not agree with that?" his squinty, barky eyes
drilled into my own. peering into the essence
of whom i was. "so, let me know, show me,
& we can determine how to move the examination forward.
would you want me to treat you incorrectly?
would you?" his voice harsh now.
lost in it all the professional guise.

"i get it."

"get what?"

"you d—on't want to help."

"what do you mean?"

"you just want to …
i don't have to sit here & take this,
not now, not—
                    not —
      not …"

my mind drivels. fuzzy edges, all blur & bloom.
a bright glared scythe along the sides
of my peripheral. outlying eclipse.
he must have noticed the change in my eyes, the glaze.

"admit it. stop pretending to be something you are not.
something that nobody is. i want to help, i really do,
but no one is buying this shit. no amount of word magic
will make me believe you know your body better than i do.
better than a physician, better than someone's whose job is
bodies."

thoughts swirled. Mr. Padlo grabbed the back of the chair
i was sitting in & dragged it around.
pushed it so my knees buckled tight to the front of his desk.

eyes blinking rapidly.

rapidly.

rapidly— all my worries swelled to the surface,
but with no focus … i … i … hand slapped over the skin
on my neck. over the bump.

Mr. Padlo sat down across from me.
that stethoscope slipping down the left side of his chest.
"man to man, Ashton. okay?" i glanced at him,
then back to the shifting flashes encroaching my vision.
"i think we should have a conversation
about how the real world works." he cleared his throat,
fist in front of his lips. i leeched closer to the back of the chair,
squirmed in my confusion & rush of panic.
"sit up straight."

i undid my back of its whorl. even pulled the chair in,
then found my hands under the wood.
fingerprints flat on the undersurface.

"good, see isn't that easy. to just be natural.
straight back, straight life. you aren't fooling anyone
with this whole gimmick. especially when you won't even commit.
i request a simple thing & you can't do it.
because you know, you know that would invalidate
the whole show you try to put out into the world.
it just ain't working."

so flat, knuckles arched to allow more pressure.
how the prints soaked in the wood. i could feel my whole body
channeled.
all my energy into my hands.

"now, i understand, i'm sure you've experienced trauma
& maybe a person like me failed you in the past.
we failed as a society to let it get this far."

& that's when the grinding started.
this scraping. dragged my fingernails along the underside.
all my force. a stressed caressing. nails splintered,
tiny crackles at first, then with more & more movement,
full chunks. cuticle peeling back, folded onto itself.
exposed what's underneath.

"or maybe you've failed yourself by letting it this far.
Dr. Reynolds is at fault too & i'll address that with her too.
everyone that turns a blind eye to your perversion."

blood seepage. little pools disturbed.
more scraping, more scraping.
worked a groove. into the pink interior of the nails.
a single drip onto my knee.

"Mr. Reed, if i had to give you a diagnosis:
i'd say that all your delusions directly come from this refusal
to accept reality. you were born a man &
you need to accept that. it's simple.
nature is never wrong."

the carnage. all the skin pulled back;
wood tongued away the muscle.
absorbed the blood
like so much rain.

like the mahogany remembered
what it was like during a storm.

i couldn't stop myself.
more & more scraping.

"it really breaks my heart."

fingers turned to rubbish, worn-away mess.
grinded down any distinction of me.
i couldn't stop myself. an erosion.
more pressure.
i had to keep my face from showing
any sign of discomfort.
i couldn't stop myself.

"to think of all the damage that society
has done to you. let you think this is normal,
let you continue down this path.
it's this culture, i tell you."

the shocking of joints.
all the way up the distal.
just a fluttered mess of flesh.
i couldn't stop myself.

like my ligaments all ruptured,
the pain vanished. a numbness swell.

i couldn't stop myself.

"so i say this in the kindest way possible,
you will never, ever recover from this fake pain,
these fake diseases & infections & whatever,
if you don't stop to really understand your body.
though, you don't know shit about your own body
& that's the reason—"
i couldn't stop myself. i couldn't stop myself. i couldn't stop myself.
i couldn't stop myself. i couldn't stop myself. i couldn't stop myself.
i couldn't stop myself. wait—

"what did you say?" i replied.
no, that's not right. i knew who i was!
i knew my body … i knew … my body …
"my mental health, whatever it is, has nothing to do
with me knowing my body. me knowing … uh,
me knowing …"
      when a cocoon erupts, its defense goes with it.
        & something always emerges.
like stressed gauze, coming apart fiber by fiber.
i couldn't— my body couldn't thread itself back together.
the filaments of myself drifting in the sickly air.
that calming sickly, ginger throated, carbonated
stomach sickly. my hands hooked, trembling,
fingers couldn't grasp at any of me floating away

"excuse me?"

"none of this means i don't know my own body.
i know this body. i know who i am."
             i told you.

"i told you …"

"told me what?"

??:?? P??????????????????????

"i told you. i know.

who i am.

i have   always   known
who i am.

i don't need   anyone   else
telling me
about my body,

telling me if this body
is right,
or if this body

is wrong.

no one else   can tell me
who i am.
i can be selfish,
i can be weak.

i don't need
to be anything.

i don't need to be

                                   y

                       n

                                       t

                                             h   n

                                                   i

             a

                                                             g

                                          for anyone.

i know   this body. i know
       this body …"

that's right …

i know this body.

??:?? ???

& i need to trust this body.

i need to trust this body.   i need to trust this body.
i need to trust this body.   i need to trust this body.
i need to trust this body.   i need to trust this body.
i need to trust this body.   i need to trust this body.
i need to trust this body.   i need to trust this body.
i need to trust this body.   i need to trust this body.
i need to trust this body.   i need to trust this body.
i need to trust this body.   i need to trust this body.
i need to trust this body.   i need to trust this body.
i need to trust this body.   i need to trust this body.
... i need to trust this body.   i need to trust — body.
  i need to trust this body.   i need to trust this body.

  i need to trust this body.   i need to trust this body.
    i need to trust this body.   i need to trust this body.
      i need to trust this body.   i need ... trust this body.
        i need to — this body.   i need to trust this body.
          i need to trust this body.   i need to trust this body.
            i need to trust this body.   i need to trust this body.
              i need to trust this body. i need to trust this body.
                i need ... this body.— trust this body.
                    i need to —

  i needed to listen to my body.

      it was mine.   it was mine.

  trust it to warn me of danger.

                                              blink.

  & not the other way around.

??:?9 ?????????????

a paradigm shift.

the pain from the neck escaped & a surge of anxious energy
rippled through my body & then i heard it.

an ambulatory alarm. this guttural reverberation in the same tone,
cadence of Dr. Reynolds but otherworldly. not her, but her.

i couldn't move what was left of my fingers.
nubs of runny meat.
the pain welling rheum at the corner
of my eyelids. my grip all
but gone under this dull prickling,
like numbness. i craned
my head back to see Mr. Padlo's grin.

that alabaster shit-eating grin.

not even paying any attention
to the blood easing its way onto the floor.

corneal sockets clear of their eyes,
an empty skull. ovoid blackness.

more skeleton than man.
more man than ever before.

"&, um, fuck you Mr. Padlo
for not believing me."

a beginning.

??:0? ?????

slammed the door open, frame shudder & dent.
into the hallway, this darkness
between flashes of red. a strobe. my eyes
opened but still pinned tight, a tunnel.

i felt so much better.

i had stood up for myself.
peering down, my hands quivered.
so run down, muscles showing through each tip.

a light pain in my teeth.
heartbeat rubbed worn the skin.

i put my finger under my nose.
my breathing.

i felt so much   better.
                    i stood up
                    for myself.

eyes adapted. pupils calculated the space.
where could Dr. Reynolds be?
she was there in that room with me.

i started walking. running. sprinting. every four steps,
felt like two. the walls tightened,
constricting around me, a lung of concrete & plywood.

i had no clue where i was going.

is this what it feels like?
                was that a breakthrough?
another shout. her voice closer & farther.
an obscured direction. before everything looked familiar.
like the hospital i've been to so many times but now,
it's all different. the paint, the loose supplies,
the smell, how this turn moves into that corner
into that corner into that room.

this felt so off. weird. extra dimensional.
supernatural, i don't know.

like the space has taken it upon itself
to change alongside me.

body turned. the same. snap,
change direction. the same.

hush.

0?:?? ?M

& my body froze.
misty silence.

i listened to my body & my body
was telling me that something was coming.

heard soft footsteps. no, harder. more force.
could it be that person?

> *no, we looked at that logically, Ashton,*
> *like you wanted.*

that's right.

doesn't change my sense of dread, this bead
of sweat crest next to my eyelid.

ready to drip. ready to alert whatever it is
to my presence. i could only imagine turning around
to two red eyes, currant glow—

my neck throbbed. i smacked it down.
this sort of hummingbird sound.
insanely fast pitter-patter.

the steps were getting closer.
pressure wasn't soothing the neck
because my fingers couldn't apply any.

they were worthless then. my hands
were worthless, my body kept telling me.

… turning around to jowls, a pair of fist-like palps
covering the mouth, proboscis dangling, broken open,
secreted saliva stringing great feathers like antennae.
taste of metal, a grinding sound. a retching—

Ashton!

listen to my body. blink.

… turning to flashes of a bulge from my neck growing.
toad's throat mastication. the pain i felt pushed down
with my mushy fingertips. a conduction of sound
from my slivers of visible bone.
the pain i felt. suddenly—

"Ashton! oh thank god, i found you."

… turning to a maze. a labyrinth of seafoam
mildew coated stone—

"oh god, your hands, Ashton …"

my consciousness waffled, a series of blinks.
into & out of darkness. my back teeth
ensnared the fat inside my mouth
between them … turning to a vibration.

brought my body down. fear overwhelmed.
arms lost strength. the throbbing extended.
my shoulders seared, back grasped.

"it's okay, it's okay."

… turned to being pulled. wholeness
being sucked away. my clothes wet, second skinned.
tongue dried, prickly. voice all gone;
tissues recoiled expiration. no tension, no sound,
no clearing, a cough.

"we need to treat you."

another cough.

"please, come on."

blink.

turned around & there was Dr. Reynolds.
her latexed hands covering mine,
holding down the oozing with small towel.

i yelped out in pain, which must
have shocked her because she dropped my hands
& took a step back. a humming resonance.

timbre of coming to.

"i'm sorry, i didn't mean to, Ashton, are you okay?"

"Dr. Reynolds ..."

"no, are you okay?"

"i thought i was, i had this moment,
i didn't feel the dying, but then
all of a sudden, it turned."

"your hands are severely wounded,
so that makes sense. your body is telling you."

"my body?"

"yes, please, let's get back
& we'll take care of it. you'll be fine."

"i'll be fine."

i'll be fine.

                                                            bli   n
                                                                  k.

                                              i'll be fine.
i'll be fine. i'll be fine. i'll be fine.

                        i'll be fine. i'll be fine.

            i'll be fine.
i'll be fine i'll be fine
            i'll be fine i'll be fine i'll be fine i'll be fine

i
l
b
e
f
i
n
e
i
l
l
b
e
f
i
n
e
i
l
l
b
e
f
i
n
e

i
l
l
b
e
f
i
n
e

illbefineillbefinefinefinefinefinefinefinefinefinefinefineillbefinefinefi
nefinefinefinefinefinefinefinefinefinefinefinefinefinefine
finefinefinefineillbefine

i wanted to blink

b
u
t
i'
ll
b
e
fi
n
e
.

fine.

195

& for the first time in a long time, i believed that.

i felt it in my body.

03:55 PM

"so, keep those wrapped for a few hours, at least.
i think we can monitor them over the next week.
there was some minor tissue damage, but you are lucky,
it's not as bad as we both, i'm sure, originally thought."
Dr. Reynolds & i were walking back to the lobby.
bandaged hands. buddy-taping. she mentioned support.
my vision had been fuzzy, a refusal to see the wound.
both of us fixated on my fingers as to not see anything else.
"you've lost some muscle mass, but overall
we are in the clear there."

"right, i get it." my voice picked clean, monotone-sound-wave.

"here's the lobby," her hand flattened out,
turned to show the way, the right lobby, "don't hesitate
to contact my nursing team, the number is on those post-exam
forms if you have any questions
or if something starts to look a-miss.
especially in terms of an infection."

"thank you ..."

dejected creature all in all, but
i'm not sure i'd need that.
the way i was in tune with my body.
these fingers were no problem.
even though they may be worthless for a while.
little swelling, compress, sensitivity, stiffness,

but i had the whole treatment down. couple stitches,
that's it. i listened to her & i knew
how my body should react from there on.

i lifted my arm & elbowed the door open.
Dr. Reynolds waved at me while i walked into the lobby
& the door swung close. everything looked normal,
if quiet still. i gazed over at Mabel, talking on the phone,
behind the counter. she smiled at me
as i made my way to the exit.

i'll be fine.

like that, the automatic doors burst open.
frigid air flapped over my dressings;
the pain twitched my lips
as i curled my fingers in pain..

my body continually healing. continually working itself
so i don't have to suffer.

i'll be fine.

04:06 PM

the parking lot felt expansive. a desert.
a hot, gloomy mirage.

nearing my car, i noticed my shoelaces
untied & my balance
off-kilter & i tripped on the plastic lace tip
caught under my foot.
my body skittered across the gravel
& when i pushed myself back up,
i saw an abrasion
on my knee. this crosshatched scrape.

i'll be fine.

a trickle of blood pulled down, mooring
onto my calf. completely back on my feet now,
balanced, situated,
my breathing shallow— i'll be fine.

i could see pebble fragments,
a dusty wheeze. the skin around
my knee roughed black.

i'll b—

lowered my hand to the wound
& smudged away some blood
with my wrist. when i looked at it closely,

i saw debris. excess that shouldn't be in me.
i needed to clean it out. i couldn't let it
get it infected, could i?
it could lead to …

                                        —link

i turned back towards the hospital.
the bright ER sign flashing

like a welcome signal. a warmth.

blink.

ACKNOWLEDGEMENTS

thanks to you for reading.

thanks to Heather and Steve from Brigids Gate Press for believing that this book deserves to exist.

thanks to Joe Koch, Hailey Piper, and Nick Cutter for the constant inspiration and for blessing this book with such kind words.

thanks to Stephanie Ellis for your dedication, time, and patience.

thanks to Jonathan Koven for the sincere feedback; this book, especially the ending, would not be the same without you.

thanks to all of my friends and family for supporting me every single day.

ABOUT THE AUTHOR

luna rey hall is a queer trans non-binary writer. they are the author of *space neon neon space* (Variant Lit, 2022), *no matter the diagnosis* (Game Over Books, 2023), *the patient routine* (Brigids Gate Press, 2023), and *loudest when startled* (YesYes Books, 2020), longlisted for the 2020 Julie Suk Award. they are the winner of the 2013 Patsy Lea Core in Memorial Award for Poetry. their poems have appeared in *The Florida Review*, *The Rumpus*, & *Raleigh Review*, among others. find more at lunareyhall.com.

About the Illustrator

Elizabeth Leggett is a Hugo award-winning illustrator whose work focuses on soulful, human moments-in-time that combine ambiguous interpretation and curiosity with realism.

Much to her mother's dismay, she viewed her mother's whitewashed walls as perfectly good canvasses so she believes it is safe to say that she has been an artist her whole life! Her first published work was in the Halifax County Arts Council poetry and illustration collection. If she remembers correctly, she was not yet in double digits yet, but she might be wrong about that. Her first paying gig was painting other students' tennis shoes in high school.

In 2012, she ended a long fallow period by creating a full seventy-eight card tarot in a single year. From there, she transitioned into freelance illustration. Her clients represent a broad range of outlets, from multiple Hugo award winning Lightspeed Magazine to multiple Lambda Literary winner, Lethe Press. She was honored to be chosen to art direct both Women Destroy Fantasy and Queers Destroy Science Fiction, both under the Lightspeed banner.

Elizabeth, her husband, and their typically atypical cats, live in New Mexico. She suggests if you ever visit the state, look up. The skies are absolutely spectacular.

Content Warnings

Mental illness
Excessive violence
Death/dying
Suicide/self-harm
Transphobia

MORE FROM BRIGIDS GATE PRESS

Prepare for adventure as Juliana, a nineteen-year-old Brazilian, finds herself forced to run from an occult overlord, leaving her sister in peril. Temporarily safe, Juliana works to save money for Vilma's rescue—and along the way, meets Patrick, a rich-boy mountain climber with friends in high places.

Angus Addison wants to see his corporate flag on the summit of Mount Everest—carried there by the first woman in history—but the Himalayas are no joke. Failure could cost both sisters their lives.

Juliana weighs the risks and rewards—for even if she raises the cash, she still must figure a way to free Vilma from the same man she ran from—a man known to his disciples as The Farmer.

Who are we if not for the monsters that we keep?

They Hide: Short Stories to Tell in the Dark collects thirteen chilling tales that weave through the shadows, exploring the nature of fear, powerlessness, and control.

- A series of murders in a New England colony
- An untamed beast in pre-revolutionary France
- A mysterious stranger who invades 18th-century Ireland
- A traveling circus that takes more than the price of admission
- A gathering of the Dark, telling tales on the longest night of the year, and more.

Come play with vampires, werewolves, ghosts, zombies, ghouls and the devil himself. Make sure you check under the bed and don't turn out the lights.

The settlement of Grey's Bluffs is a prosperous town. An independent community dwelling in the shadows of the mountains known only as The Hungers.
Esther Foxman and Siobhan O'Clery have grown up in Grey's Bluffs, thriving out on the western territories in the aftermath of the Civil War. Devoted to one another and their home, the two set out to complete a regular pact at the Hungers to ensure that Grey's Bluffs continues to prosper.

Cyril Redstone is a man who knows death well. Becoming a mercenary after the Civil War, Cyril leads the marauding Blackhawks from one slaughter to the next. Hired to destroy Grey's Bluffs, Cyril cares little for morality, nor that he owes its founder his life.

Esther and Siobhan are left to defend the only home they have ever known from the Blackhawks, their confrontation driving them deep into the mountains.

Where the darkest secrets of the Hungers await them.

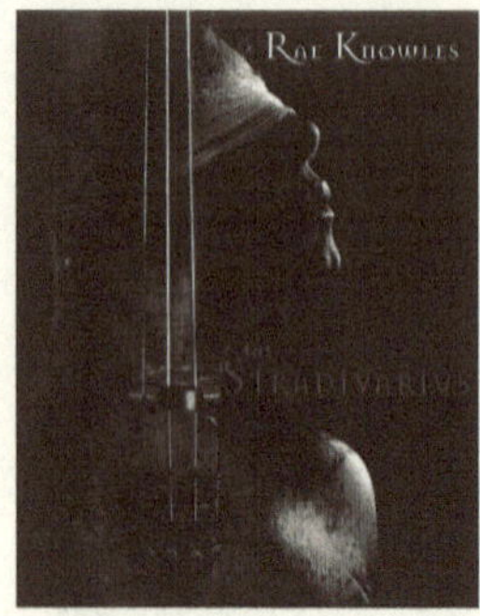

When a surprise inheritance and whirlwind romance offer Mae a chance to escape her repressive aunt, she's all too eager to elope and start life anew in her childhood home. But when she and her new husband arrive, the towering Victorian sits in disrepair, and Mae learns that her father's decade-old, unsolved murder is still a source of rumor and speculation in town.

Leading the charge to unravel the mystery surrounding her father's death is Ollie, a vibrant genderqueer and an outsider in their hometown. Sure that solving the cold case will land them a coveted job in the police department, Ollie gains access to the Victorian by agreeing to do maintenance work on the property

Inside, Mae is taunted by a feminine specter, soft voices from empty rooms, and distinct melodies of Lady Paola: the priceless, Stradivarius violin stolen the night of her father's murder.

Forte, mezzo-forte, the measured, andante cadence.

Her hiss, her pull, her scream.

Mae fears the house is haunted by her father's spirit, her husband believes she's going the way of her mother—slipping into madness, but Ollie suspects something more sinister is at play.

If Ollie and Mae can't work together to uncover the Victorian's secrets, Mae will join her mother in an institution or her father in the grave.

Visit our website at: www.brigidsgatepress.com